Secrets and Sequins

A Ghostly Fashionista Mystery

Gayle Leeson

Grace Abraham Publishing
Bristol, Virginia

Gayle Leeson/Grace Abraham Publishing
13335 Holbrook Street, Suite 10
Bristol, Virginia 24202
www.gayleleeson.com

Publisher's Note: This is a work of fiction. Names, characters, places, and incidents are a product of the author's imagination. Locales and public names are sometimes used for atmospheric purposes. Any resemblance to actual people, living or dead, or to businesses, companies, events, institutions, or locales is completely coincidental.

Cover design by Wicked Smart Designs.

Book Layout ©2017 BookDesignTemplates.com

Ordering Information:
Quantity sales. Special discounts are available on quantity purchases by corporations, associations, and others. For details, contact the "Special Sales Department" at the address above.

Secrets and Sequins/Gayle Leeson. -- 1st ed.

Dedicated to Tim, Lianna, and Nicholas

Chapter One

I glanced up from pinning a strand of sequins on the bodice of a pink satin gown when the door to my workshop opened. Customers came into the shop through the reception area, so I knew this would be another Shops on Main vendor or a friend. Or both, as I considered the vendors my friends—except for Jason, the photographer whose studio was upstairs. He was more than a friend.

My smile broadened as Zoe came into the room. I'd met Zoe when I'd done the costumes for *Beauty and the Beast* for her high school, and now she worked for me part-time. The blue-haired teen had quite an eye for fashion and had thrown herself into making masks for the upcoming masquerade ball, many of which matched the dresses I was making.

The smile faltered slightly when I saw Maggie, Zoe's mother, walking in behind her. Maggie didn't particularly like the fact that Zoe spent so much time here at Designs on You with me and her great-aunt—or would that be great-*great*-aunt—Max. Maggie's dad, Dwight, also spent quite a bit of time hanging out with me and his dead aunt.

So Max was a ghost. But she wasn't a spooky, chain-rattling ghost. Although, I'm pretty sure that if she'd had some necklaces, she'd have rattled them if she could. She didn't have the ability to touch anything, but she could manipulate electronics like nobody's business. Since meeting me when I'd opened the shop, she'd been introduced to e-books, movies, and social media. She loved it. She said she hadn't felt so alive in over eighty years.

My grandfather—Grandpa Dave—and I, and my dad could see and hear Max because the love of her life was related to us. Of course, Dwight, Zoe, and Maggie could see and hear Max because they were family. As far as we knew, no one else could interact with Max and vice versa.

Maggie had made it abundantly clear that she had no desire to get to know Max. Of course, Maggie didn't want to get to know me any better either. Granted, I had found myself involved in a murder investigation or two…or three…since opening my shop, but the murders weren't my fault; and I only got involved in the investigations because I seemed to have a knack for sleuthing.

Zoe carefully closed the door once she and Maggie were inside. I had notes on both doors requesting that they be kept closed so that Jasmine, "Jazzy," my gray and white tabby, didn't escape the shop and possibly wind up running out into the busy street in front of Shops on Main.

"Hi, Zoe." I popped the pin I was holding back onto the pincushion I wore on my wrist. "Maggie, nice to see you."

Maggie nodded. "Is she here?"

Zoe huffed. "She isn't, Mom. If Max was here, you'd see her." Turning to me, she said, "I wanted to show Mom the masks I've been making."

"Great." Addressing Maggie, I added, "She's done an impressive job."

"It's all she talks about lately at home," Maggie said. "It's a new school year, and I've told her she'd better keep her grades up if she wants to keep working here."

"If it's okay with you, Zoe, I'm going to step out onto the porch for a bit of fresh air since you're here."

"That's cool."

I strolled through the reception area and out onto the porch. There was a bench swing at one end, and I took a seat.

"She didn't get that snooty attitude from Dot. I'll tell you that right now." Max appeared on the swing beside me. "It must've been on her daddy's side."

I started to suggest that Maggie's attitude could've come from her great-aunt Max, but I wisely held my tongue. "Where have you been?"

"Just resting. With you being here all hours of the day and night lately, I have to go away when I feel my energy waning, so I'll be here if and when you need me."

I had no idea where Max went to rest, and I wasn't sure she did either. All we knew was that she'd died falling down the stairs in the main hallway, was tethered to this building, and had no idea why she hadn't moved on. Selfishly, I was glad she was still here.

"She just burns me up." Max continued ranting about Maggie. "*Is she here*? I heard her say that, and I'm glad Zoe put her in her place. That Zoe, now there's a child after my own heart. Dwight too. But Maggie—?" She sighed and shook her head.

Max couldn't fool me. I knew she was eager for Maggie to talk to her and allow Max to get to know her.

"Hopefully, she'll come around," I said.

"Yeah, well, whether she does or not is no skin off my beak, but she'd better tell Zoe those masks she's made are the elephant's eyebrows because they are!"

Connie came outside and joined me on the swing. In fact, she practically sat on Max.

Rubbing her hands up and down her arms, she said, "I got a chill."

Max gave her a little wave, rolled her eyes, and went through the wall into Designs on You.

"Well, it *is* mid-September," I said.

"I do love autumn." She smiled, as she pushed the swing with her sandaled feet. "I saw you through the window, and it appeared you were talking to yourself. You really need to give yourself a break, kiddo."

"I know. I just keep going over and over what I still need to do before the ball."

Money was good, but I was glad I didn't have to keep up this pace for much longer. I'd been busier than usual for the past six weeks or so, but the past two weeks had been insane. I was working around the clock putting finishing touches on custom gowns, customizing dresses my clientele had bought from my ready-to-wear line, and making alterations.

"Is there anything I can do to help?" Connie asked.

Connie owned Delightful Home, the shop directly across the hall from Designs on You. She sold scented candles, essential oils, tea blends, soaps, and lotions. She was calm and artsy—you might call her bohemian if you meant it in the very nicest way.

"I truly appreciate the offer, but other than Zoe making the masks, I'm on my own."

Tucking a strand of her long hair behind her ear, Connie said, "She has really shown a knack for fashion, hasn't she? First the hats for the Renaissance Festival, and now these masks. I'm glad she's found such a wonderful mentor in you."

"Thank you. I—" I broke off, chuckling at the site of Grandpa Dave parking his white pickup truck on the street.

Connie smiled. "What luck! He got a terrific spot."

I stopped the swing and went to meet Grandpa Dave. He took a Dutch oven carrier out of the passenger seat.

"Hey, Pup!" He nodded toward the swing. "Hi, there, Connie!"

"Hi, Dave!"

I kissed his cheek. "Do you need me to take that?"

"No, I've got it. It's heavy. I need to make sure my best girl is getting fed."

"Chicken and dumplings?" I guessed.

"You've got it."

We climbed the stairs, and Connie held the door open for us.

"I was telling Amanda you got lucky with that parking space," she said.

"I'm an incredibly lucky man." He winked. "Would you like some chicken and dumplings?"

"I wish. I have to go home and make dinner for the family." Connie was married to Will, and they had two children.

"Maybe Will will surprise you and have it ready when you get there," I said.

"Maybe. Or one of us could get takeout. We usually save that for Fridays, but this has been an unusually busy Thursday."

We all went inside. Connie returned to Delightful Home, and Grandpa Dave and I went into my shop where we found Max playing with Jazzy in the reception area while Maggie and Zoe remained in the workroom, or atelier, looking at Zoe's handiwork.

"Good afternoon, Silver Fox," Max had taken her nickname for Grandpa Dave from a term she'd heard from "the jewelry gal" who used to have a shop upstairs.

"How's my favorite flapper?" he asked.

"I would say *unflappable*." She jerked her head in the direction of the atelier. "But I'm *flapped*."

He grinned. "It'll be all right."

"I'm beginning to wonder." Max rolled her eyes.

Grandpa Dave took the Dutch oven carrier through to the kitchen. I heard Zoe greet him enthusiastically.

"What happened?" I asked Max softly.

"Not much. I went into the workroom, Zoe said hello and began telling me about her day, and Maggie ignored me. When she turned her back, I stuck my tongue out at her—entirely for Zoe's amusement—and then I came in here to play with Jazzy." She looked down at the tabby, who was looking up at her adoringly. "You love me, don't you, darling?"

"We all love you. Maggie will too, if she ever lets herself."

Zoe came sprinting into the reception area. "I'm gonna call Papaw and see if he'd like to come join us for chicken and dumplings. And then I'm supposed to ask the other vendors if they'd like some."

"Is Maggie staying?" I asked.

"No. She has to go to work. I'll go back home with Papaw."

"Sounds great." I knew Grandpa Dave usually made enough chicken and dumplings to feed the proverbial small army; but even without Connie and Maggie, there would be a pretty big crowd. I wasn't as worried about having enough food as I was about us having enough room for everyone in our kitchen.

Once he'd put the pot of chicken and dumplings on to simmer in the kitchen, Grandpa Dave came back and joined Max and me.

"Thank you for dinner." I hugged him. "I appreciate your thoughtfulness, and I'm glad you're going to be eating with me tonight. I've missed seeing you lately."

He sighed. "Unfortunately, I won't be joining you this evening. I have plans with Monica."

"Ugh, I'd forgotten *she* was back," Max said. "She's been gone so long, and we've been doing so well without her." She shrugged.

"I'll stop in and see you when I bring Monica back to get her car," he said.

As he left the shop to go upstairs and get Monica, Max stomped her foot. "I don't like that woman."

"I know."

Monica owned a collectibles shop, and she and Grandpa Dave had been dating. A month ago, Monica's daughter-in-law had broken her leg, and Monica had gone to Nebraska to help out the family. She'd returned a couple of days ago.

"Mark my words," Max said. "That woman is going to cause some trouble around here—sooner rather than later."

Chapter Two

That evening after Zoe, Dwight, Jason, Ford—from Antiquated Editions—and I had eaten our fill of Grandpa Dave's chicken and dumplings and I'd put the remainder in the refrigerator, Grandpa Dave and Monica returned to get her car. I was the only one left at Shops on Main, and I had the doors locked. Connie, mother hen that she could be, had insisted on it for my safety. She didn't realize I usually had a "watch ghost" who kept me apprised of everything going on in or around the building. But even Max had faded out and had gone to rest tonight, and Jazzy was snoring softly on her bed.

A tap on the window alerted me that Grandpa Dave was outside. I went to the door and let him in.

"Hi, there." I gave him a tired smile.

"Hey, Pup. You look beat. Are you about ready to call it a night?"

"Almost."

"It's awfully quiet in here." He gazed around the shop. "Where's Max?"

"She needed some rest," I said. "She was fading fast." Blowing out a breath, I added, "So am I."

"Not to sound like an old grandpa or anything, but if you're going to take on this much work in the future, you need to hire more help."

"I know. But this masquerade ball is an unusual occurrence. This is what—the twenty-fifth anniversary of the Brea Ridge Historical Society? I shouldn't have to do this again for another quarter of a century." I gave a half-hearted laugh. "Did you and Monica have a good time?"

"We did." He shoved his hands in his pockets. "So, uh, is Maggie coming around?"

Shaking my head, I said, "Hardly. This was the first time she's been in the building since Mom and Dad were visiting back in the summer."

"She hasn't even talked with Max since then?" he asked.

"No. Poor Max. It really hurts her feelings."

"I know. But keep in mind that Max *is* a ghost—a wonderful person and a terrific friend, but a spirit, nonetheless. That's a big pill for anyone to swallow, especially someone like Maggie—widowed at a young age, a single mom, caretaker to her father."

"Dwight doesn't need a caretaker." I finished pinning up the hem of a dress I had on a mannequin. "He does just fine on his own."

"True, but that doesn't keep Maggie from making herself responsible for him. I believe she feels as if Dwight and Zoe are the carefree children, if you will, and that she has to be the taskmaster who looks out for both of them."

"I guess." I stood back to make sure the hem was straight.

"The point I'm trying to make is that Maggie is a pragmatist. She knows Max is real but has a hard time wrapping her head around that fact and coming to terms with the fact that something she can't understand can still be a good thing." He nodded toward the mannequin. "Looks great. Are you ready to call it a night?"

"Yes."

"Good. I'll load Jazzy into her carrier."

"Thanks." I narrowed my eyes. "What's going on?" Not that it was out of character for Grandpa Dave to help me any way he could, but I had a feeling that he was rushing us out of Shops on Main for a reason.

"Nothing. I simply thought I'd see you home."

It wasn't until we got to my house and were sitting on the sofa with mugs of Connie's kava tea that I learned what Grandpa Dave wanted to talk with me about and why he wasn't keen to do so at the shop.

"Monica really enjoyed spending time with her family in Nebraska these past few weeks." He took a sip of his tea as if he were simply making casual conversation. "She's considering closing her shop and moving there." Another sip. "She's even asked me if I'd like to go with her—at least, for a couple of months to see how I like the place."

My jaw dropped. "You're kidding."

"No, she…she really asked me to go."

"But you can't! Y-you hardly know this woman. And you've never lived anywhere but here. You'd hate moving to a new place."

"Never say never, Pup. It's true I've never lived anywhere else, but it might be high time I have a change of scenery."

"Grandpa, are you seriously considering *marrying* this woman and moving halfway across the country?"

He held up one hand in protest. "Now, settle down. All I'm doing at the moment is mulling over her offer. Heck, she might even change her mind about going. I wanted your thoughts on the matter, that's all." He inclined his head. "I guess I got 'em."

There was a tug of war going on in my brain. On one side was reason and logic and a million and forty-five reasons that Grandpa Dave should not leave Abingdon to go traipsing off to Nebraska with a woman he barely knew. On the other side was selfishness, and it was telling me I should let Grandpa do whatever he wanted the way he'd always supported me in everything I'd ever done.

I took a deep breath. "I'm sorry, Grandpa. Of course, I want you to do what's best for you, and I'll support you in that decision no matter what it is."

"Thanks, Pup." He patted my hand.

I could hardly wait to tell Max how right she was about Monica.

Since Max was likely still resting and I needed to talk with someone immediately about Grandpa Dave potentially losing his mind, I called Dad.

"Dad, Grandpa Dave just left, and he has lost his mind!" I shouted as soon as he answered.

"Good evening to you too! Your mom and I are fine and, in case you were wondering, perfectly sane—as far as we know."

"Sorry. I'm just upset."

"So I gathered," he said. "Now calmly tell me what's going on."

"He's talking about moving to Nebraska with Monica."

"Fair enough. He *is* losing his mind. I'll call him and find out—"

"Don't," I interrupted. "I don't want him to know I've talked with you about it. Let him tell you on his own."

"Okay." He drew out the word.

"I suppose I wanted to vent more than anything and to get your opinion on why he'd even entertain the notion of moving so far away. You and Mom moved for your job. I understood that, but *this*?"

"Let me ask you something. If Jason got a job in California and asked you to marry him and move with him, would you do it?"

That question hit me hard. "I-I don't know. There are so many things to consider. I'd have to leave Grandpa Dave and Max and Zoe and Dwight and my business and my friends and my customers." I gulped. "Or else I'd lose Jason."

"Maybe that's exactly what your grandpa is going through."

For a moment, I couldn't speak. My throat had closed, and tears were dripping off my chin.

"Whatever choice he makes, it'll be all right, Princess," he said softly.

"B-but I don't want him to leave!" How Dad understood what I was saying through my blubbering was beyond me, but he did.

"I know." He tried to lighten the mood. "You didn't carry on like this when your mom and I left."

"I did," I said. "You just didn't know it."

"It was hard to leave you too."

I sniffled. "What should I do?"

"Love and support him. That's all you *can* do."

"I love you, Dad."

"I love you too, Princess. Now, tell me how everything is going with regard to this masquerade ball coming up on Saturday. I wish I could be there. I do love a good party."

For the next half hour, I regaled Dad with stories of customers and their dress requests, Zoe's masks, and Max's wishing for a change of venue from the Brea Ridge Fairgrounds main building to Shops on Main. But my concern about Grandpa Dave making a move he wasn't—or I wasn't—ready for remained in the back of my mind.

Chapter Three

Max was furious when I told her Grandpa Dave was considering moving to Nebraska with Monica.

"Oooh! I'm gonna haunt her! I'm going up there as soon as she gets here, and I'm going to haunt the daylights out of her!"

"What good will that do?" I put kibble and water into Jazzy's bowls before returning to the kitchen to make a pot of coffee. Shops on Main wouldn't be open for another couple of hours, and I was the only person—live person—there. I'd been in early every morning this week.

"It'll do me some good," Max said. "I told you that Monica was trouble. I knew it from the first time I set my peepers on that dame."

"I have to admit, part of me would love for you to haunt her. But Grandpa said she hadn't made up her mind about leaving yet." I inhaled the rich aroma of coffee and willed the beverage to hurry and brew. "If you haunt her, you might aid in making the decision to get out of Abingdon."

"Ugh. I hadn't thought of that." She sighed. "I do want her to leave, but she absolutely can't take Dave with her. She can't!"

"I feel the same way." I told her about my conversation with Dad.

Anchoring her fists to her hips, she said, "I'm gonna give that palooka what for the next time I talk with him. How dare he make this whole situation seem faintly plausible and not about *us*?"

I smiled as I poured a mug full of coffee. "I feel you. I was on the verge of hysterics when I called Dad, and he made me understand what a difficult position Grandpa Dave is in. All I can do is try not to make it harder on him."

"Yeah, I know." She perched on top of the refrigerator, crossing her arms over her chest and pouting like an overgrown flapper version of Tinker Bell. "But I can snoop on that Monica and see if she's up to anything nefarious."

"Thanks. I appreciate that." Sure, I was mainly humoring Max. And I doubted Monica was behaving suspiciously, but I certainly did want to know if she was.

Fortunately, I'd gotten quite a bit done and was feeling pleased with the progress I'd made when Renata Crenshaw blustered into Designs on You. Ms. Crenshaw was president of the Brea Ridge Historical Society, and it was ever so important to her that people realize how critical, how busy, and how vital to the success of the upcoming masquerade ball she was.

"Amanda, *darling*, I intended to get by here last week for my final fitting, but I've been swamped. I don't know why the historical society even has all those committees when I'm still expected to sign off on everything—and by *sign off* I mean *do*." She gave an airy laugh.

Grateful Max had taken off for the time being, I forced out a laugh of my own and retrieved Ms. Crenshaw's yellow dress from the clothing rack in the atelier.

"Oh, it's lovely, isn't it?" She clucked her tongue. "I do wish it had some beading around the neckline, though. Wouldn't that be exquisite? Tiny pearls perhaps?"

Since the woman was staring at me, I tried not to make it apparent that I was gritting my teeth. “I can put some beading on the neckline.”

“Would you? She clasped her hands together. “How delightful. You are a treasure, Amanda.” She reached into her purse and took out two tickets for the ball. “These are for you—a token of my immense appreciation for all the hard work you’ve been doing on my behalf and for the historical society as a whole.”

“Thank you.” I took the tickets. Payment for all the extra work I’d done on her dress would’ve been nice—I’d barely break even after all the changes she’d made—but tickets to the ball were better than nothing.

“How thrilling it will be for you to see all your exquisite creations displayed in one place!” She gave another of her trilling little laughs. “I’ll be back after lunch to pick up the dress.”

“And have your final fitting,” I reminded. *Final, as in, we’re done. Please don’t come back.*

Ms. Crenshaw breezed out the door, making me wonder if she’d even heard me. Not that it mattered—she’d do whatever she wanted anyway.

Since Jason would already be at the ball taking photographs, I called Grandpa Dave.

“Good morning, Pup.”

“Hi. Please tell me you don’t have any plans for tomorrow night.”

"Nothing I can't change. What's up?"

I explained how Renata Crenshaw had given me two tickets to the masquerade ball. "You wouldn't make me have to go alone, would you?"

"Have my best girl go stag to the social event of the season? Not on a bet!"

"Thanks, Grandpa. I'll have Zoe make you a terrific mask."

"I don't doubt that for a minute. I'd better get to rearranging my schedule."

After talking with Grandpa, I got busy sewing tiny pearl beads around the neckline of Ms. Crenshaw's chiffon gown. It was delicate work, since I had to sew each bead on by hand. I'd be lucky to get finished by the time she returned.

Thankfully, I was using a thimble, or else I'd have stabbed myself when Max startled me with a self-congratulatory *uh-huh!*

"Uh-huh, what?" I asked, annoyed that she'd sneaked up on me and scared me half out of my mind. "If I prick myself and get blood on this yellow dress, I'm gonna kill you. I mean—"

"I knew she was up to something," she said. "Dave called her while I was upstairs spying on her."

Nodding, I said, "I imagine he called to let her know he's going with me to the masquerade ball tomorrow night."

"He did. And she acted as if that was swell with her. *That's lovely, Dave,*" she mocked. "But after they spoke, she immediately called someone and was griping about it. She said—and I quote—*I have to get him out from under Amanda's thumb for this to work.* I knew she was up to no good."

"Who was she talking to?"

"Does it matter? She said what she said, and that's what counts." She shook her fist at the ceiling. "Whatever that floozy thinks she's going to pull, she's got another think coming. I'm going back up there."

I opened my mouth to speak, but Max was gone before I could say anything. Turning slightly, I looked at Jazzy, who was lying in a ray of sunshine. "What can we do?"

The cat yawned and batted at a dust mote. Since I typically read meaning into all of Jazzy's actions, particularly when I was speaking with her, I took that to indicate that there wasn't really anything we could do at that point. Still, I was rather glad Max was staking out Monica's shop.

It was nearly four p.m. when Dwight and Zoe came into Shops on Main. He poked his head inside Designs on You to say hello and then went to visit with the other vendors. Since he often used his "taxi app" to bring Zoe to work, he'd become a favorite among the vendors—especially since he typically bought something from everyone.

"Could you do me a favor?" I asked Zoe, as I put what I hoped would be my last masquerade ball dress to be picked up today into a garment bag.

"I'll do my best."

"Would you make Grandpa Dave a mask for the ball?"

She looked around to make sure Max wasn't present. "He bought tickets for him and Monica?"

I shook my head. "Renata Crenshaw gave me tickets during one of her two visits today."

Expelling a breath, she said, "That's good. Max filled me in on the whole Monica leaving situation this morning before I left for school. She's pretty upset about it."

"I know. She's upstairs spying on Monica now." I paused. "She might even be haunting her."

Zoe giggled. "What I wouldn't give to see that. Wonder how she'd do it?"

"I might mess with her computer," Max said from behind us both.

We both started, and Zoe said, "Cheese and crackers, Aunt Max! Why don't you give us coronaries?"

"Sorry." Max raised an index finger and listened. "And three…two…one."

Monica burst through the door into the atelier. "Do either of you know anything about computers?" She turned her attention to Zoe. "You. You're young. Aren't all young people experts in computer technology?"

"Not me, I'm afraid," Zoe said.

"Me either." I knew better than to look at Max. I noticed Zoe was avoiding looking in her aunt's direction too. "What's going on with it?"

"It keeps turning off and on!" Monica gave a growl of frustration.

Max's laughter tinkled near my ear.

"How weird." Zoe put her hand over her mouth. "Did you try turning it off and back on?"

"It's already doing that!"

"You could try unplugging the router." I hung the dress with the garments ready for pickup.

"Right. Well, I'll see if Ford knows anything." She stomped out of the atelier and practically slammed the door shut behind her.

"Good luck!" I called.

"Luck has nothing to do with it." Max fluffed her hair.

Zoe and I managed to hold in our laughter until we heard Monica's feet on the stairs.

"You're a sight," I said to Max.

"Only to the select few." She winked.

"So what sort of mask would you like for Dave?" Zoe asked. "And it should match yours, right?"

"I guess so."

She frowned. "You don't know what you're going to wear, do you?"

"No." I walked over to my ready-to-wear line. I'd made several dresses that would be suitable for the masquerade ball or for any other formal occasion.

"Have you worked so hard on this thing that you've gone screwy?" Max popped in front of me and pointed to something behind me. I turned to see my portrait hanging above the mantel. In the portrait that Jason took just after I'd opened my shop, I was wearing a 1930s-style bias cut emerald green evening gown with a plunging halter neckline and a back panel with pearl buttons that began at the middle of the back on each side and went to the waist.

"It's a gorgeous dress, but would it be appropriate for a fall formal?" I asked.

"If you were advising one of your clients, what would you say?" Zoe came to stand beside me.

"I'd say with black, opera-length gloves, it would look great."

"And, if we have to rub out Monica, no fingerprints," Max said.

Zoe and I both turned to look at her.

"Oh, applesauce! Let a gal have a little fun, won't you?" Max flounced over to the chair where Jazzy was lying and immediately had the cat's attention. "You still love me, don't you, darling?"

"We all love you," I said.

"She knows," Zoe said. "She just likes to hear it."

"Indeed, I do." She lifted and dropped one shoulder. "Is that so bad? I also don't want our Dave leaving us for parts unknown."

"Neither do we," I said.

"Nope." Zoe plucked a sketch pad off my desk. "We're not getting down in the dumps. We've got work to do. I need to create a mask that you can rock in that hot dress and another one for Dave. You two get over here and help me brainstorm."

For my mask, we settled on a black lace with green rhinestones in swirl patterns and clear rhinestones above the eyelid. Zoe designed Grandpa's mask as a matte black with matching green rhinestones around the eyes.

When she'd drawn both masks, she showed her concept art to Max and me. "What do you think?"

"They'll look gorgeous," I said. "Your best masks yet!"

"I just wish I could go." Max looked down at Jazzy. "You and I miss all the fun, don't we?"

Zoe's phone rang, and she hurried into the atelier to answer it. When she returned, she said, "You might get your wish, Aunt Max. Well, kind of, anyway. That was Mom calling to tell me she's going to be late tonight. Something happened with the caterer for the masquerade ball, and they needed a replacement super quick. The restaurant Mom's working for is going to be catering it now, and she wants me to help with the serving."

Chapter Four

Jason stopped by just before I closed up shop for the day. "Hello, beautiful."

I grinned. "Hi, handsome."

"How relieved are you that all the pre-masquerade ball excitement is behind you?" he asked.

"I'm delighted." I bit my lip. "But I'm afraid that saying so will jinx it, and something crazy will happen tomorrow."

"Don't think that way. Let me take you to that new restaurant, Hot Diggity. I've been hearing good things about it."

"Okay. I've heard good things too. For one thing, they're catering the ball. Zoe's mom is working there, and she called Zoe earlier today and said things fell through with the original caterer."

"Yikes. They're in for a rough time getting everything pulled together in time for the ball," he said. "Should we go somewhere else?"

"Nah, I'm sure they can handle it." I put Jazzy in her carrier. "I have to drop this little furball off at home first."

"No problem. I'll pick you up in an hour?"

"Sounds great." I gathered the carrier and my tote. "I'm going to the ball, by the way." I explained as we left Shops on Main that Renata Crenshaw had given me two tickets. "And since you'll already be there, I had to get myself another date."

He hid a smile. "Should I be worried about this other guy?"

"Oh, definitely. He's a dreamboat, and I absolutely adore him."

"I'll be sure to get some photos of you and Dave."

I laughed. "I hope to get one with you too."

"We'll make sure of it. What are you wearing?"

"The green gown you photographed me wearing—the photo hanging over my mantel."

Clutching at his heart, he whistled softly. "You sure know how to make a guy suffer. You'll knock us all dead, and I'll have to watch you dancing with everyone except me."

"Surely, you can take a break at some point during the evening. I'll be so disappointed if I don't get to dance with you."

"We'll dance." He dropped a quick kiss on my lips. "Even if it's after everyone else goes home."

Hot Diggity would have been an excellent name for a hot dog place. Hot diggity dog just goes together. In this instance, Hot Diggity was Brea Ridge's posh new restaurant, serving everything from steak to sushi, pasta to paella. Some people thought it was a little too ambitious. I was looking forward to finding out for myself.

The hostess seated us at a small intimate table near a window and handed each of us a leather-embossed menu. A candle lantern in the middle of the table provided romantic ambience.

"This is a beautiful place," I said, as I opened the menu.

"It is."

Our server arrived, introduced himself as Brody, and placed a small cutting board containing a loaf of ciabatta bread, a bread knife, and a tiny ramekin of butter on the table. After taking our drink orders, he scurried away.

"I hear Ms. Oakes might be trying to lease Monica's shop soon," I said. "She's told Grandpa she's thinking of moving to Nebraska to be near her family."

"That's not surprising," Jason said. "I kinda thought she might since she stayed with them so long. I mean, sure, I understand her daughter-in-law couldn't get around and needed the help, but Monica could've probably divided the time with someone else."

"Yeah." I fiddled with the corner of my napkin. "The bad thing is she's asked Grandpa to go with her—not just for a visit, but to *live*."

Looking at me over the top of the menu, Jason asked, "Isn't that awfully sudden? They haven't been seeing each other all that long, have they?"

"That's what I said, but Grandpa Dave said a person his age needed to move quickly." I shook my head. "I feel like it would be a mistake, though."

"Has he said he's going?"

"No. I'm struggling with what to say. Do I discourage him from following this woman halfway across the country, or do I tell him to follow his dreams?" I asked. "He's always been supportive of anything I've wanted to do. I owe him the same courtesy. But, Jason, I don't want him to go."

"Maybe you should tell him what you've just told me."

Before I could respond, Brody returned with our drinks and was ready to take our order. We asked for another moment and then turned our attention to the menus, so we'd be prepared when he came back.

Once our order was in, I was ready to revisit the topic of Grandpa Dave, but we were interrupted by someone saying, "Amanda Tucker! Is that you?"

The voice was unfamiliar, but I swiveled my head to see Tony Diggs standing practically on top of our table.

"Tony, hi!" I smiled. I hadn't seen Tony since middle school. As a matter of fact, it had been the end of the seventh-grade school year when he'd asked me to be his girlfriend. Not wanting to hurt his feelings, I'd said yes and then not communicated with him a single time over the summer. Our romance, such as it was, quickly fizzled. "Tony, this is my boyfriend, Jason Logan. Jason is a photographer. Jason, this is Tony Diggs. We attended middle school together." Best to leave out the details of our impetuous affair.

Jason stood and shook hands with Tony.

"It's Preston Diggs, Jr., actually," Tony said. "Tony is my nickname. My dad owns this restaurant."

"Really?" I almost choked on my water. Had I known Preston Diggs owned this place, I might have suggested another restaurant. Grandma Jodie had once said that Preston Diggs was more crooked than a dog's hind leg and twice as dirty. But as I didn't know the man personally, I shouldn't judge. "Congratulations on Hot Diggity catering the masquerade ball. That's quite an accomplishment."

"Yeah, well, this time we only got it because the other caterer had to drop out, but I guarantee you that next time we'll be first on their list."

"I hope so," I said.

"I *know* so." Tony punctuated his statement with a nod. "You two enjoy your meal. Amanda, good to see you."

"Thanks."

After Tony had walked away, Jason lowered his voice to say, "He's pretty sure of himself."

"Isn't he though? I hope the food lives up to the hype." I caught a glimpse of Maggie, raised my hand slightly, but she looked the other way and kept walking.

Jason had seen my wave and had followed my gaze. "She's just busy."

"Sure." I knew better. Zoe's mother thought I was a bad influence on her daughter, and she hated me.

On Saturday morning, Zoe and Dwight arrived right after I'd opened up the shop. As I gave Jazzy her kibble and fresh water, Zoe told Max what she was wearing to the ball.

"As a worker, I can't dress up like everybody else," she said, "and that suits me fine. I'll be wearing black pants and a black button-down shirt. I'll be able to blend into the background and watch everything that's going on."

"Oh, I so wish I could be there!" Max twirled around, fascinating Jazzy, who trotted over to watch.

Zoe glanced at Dwight, barely able to suppress her smile.

"Go on and tell her," Dwight said.

"Look what Papaw bought me." Zoe held up a small rectangular black device.

"That's fantastic!" Max beamed at her great-niece.

"Do you know what it is?" Dwight asked.

"I have no idea, but you both seem to think it's the elephant's eyebrows, so I thought I'd humor you." Max gave them a shrug.

Dwight and Zoe laughed.

"It's a miniature streaming camera!" Zoe giggled. "I can share the entire evening with you, Aunt Max! You'll be there the whole time."

"Hmph." Dwight crossed his arms. "I guess I'll be sitting at home by my lonesome while everybody else is having fun at the ball."

"You can join in too, Papaw. I'll be streaming from my social media chat room."

Turning down the corners of his mouth, Dwight said, "I suppose I can participate in the fun for a little while, but I do have a couple of episodes of *Death in Paradise* to catch up on."

Zoe, Max, and I laughed at Dwight for being caught out for really wanting to be "by his lonesome" all along. As we were teasing him, Tony Diggs opened the door and walked into the reception area.

As he closed the door behind him, he looked around at Zoe and Dwight. Ignoring Zoe, he introduced himself to Dwight. "Preston Diggs, Jr., but my friends call me Tony. Are you Mr. Tucker?"

"No, sir. My name's Dwight. My daughter, Maggie, just started working for your dad at Hot Diggity."

"Maggie?" Tony shook his head. "Nope. Doesn't ring a bell, but then I have a hard time keeping track of all dad's gals."

I felt my eyes widen as I looked first at Dwight and then at Zoe.

While the rest of us might have been seething on the inside, Max was expressing her anger. "I'll have you to know my niece isn't one of *anybody's* gals." She stalked over to Tony. "Who do you think you are, palooka? You're lucky I can't sock you in the kisser!"

Tony rubbed his hands together. "You keep it cold in here, don't you?"

No, you're standing nose to nose with a ghost.

"What can I do for you, Tony?" I asked.

"Any way I could get a *private* word?" He looked pointedly at Dwight and Zoe.

"Zoe, why don't you show me the masks you've been working on? Your mom said you'd done a wonderful job with them." Dwight stood, and Zoe followed him into the atelier after throwing a baleful look in Tony's direction.

"Don't worry, darling," Max said to her. "I'll stay right here and keep an eye on this sap."

"I've been thinking of you ever since we saw each other last night," he said, when he came to the mistaken conclusion that he and I were alone.

"I'm flattered, Tony, but as I told you yesterday, I have a boyfriend."

"Yeah!" Max stuck her tongue out at him. "She's got a boyfriend, and he's a good guy."

"He *is* a good guy." I inwardly groaned. Max was constantly making me forget myself. One would think that after all this time, I'd be able to tune out her commentary when I was with someone who could neither hear nor see her, but nope—not in the least.

"I didn't say he wasn't," Tony said. "But how serious is it? There's no ring on your finger. I feel like as long as there's nothing binding you to that guy, I stand a chance."

"Again, I'm very flattered—"

"I wouldn't be flattered," Max interrupted me. "I'd tell this clown to scram."

"—but I am in a committed relationship with—"

"Yeah, yeah." This time it was Tony who didn't let me finish my thought. "I hear you. Anyway, I'll see you around." He winked. "Soon."

"Oh, take a powder already!" Max shooed him out the door. "We're sick of your phony baloney!"

Grandpa Dave arrived as Max was chasing—in her own way—Tony off the porch. He was chuckling as he came into Designs on You.

"Max is certainly worked up. What's going on?"

Dwight and Zoe had returned from the atelier, and we all began talking at once about Tony.

"I can't believe that *Marlon Rando* called my mom one of his dad's *gals*," Zoe said.

"And Jason sure wouldn't appreciate how the creep wouldn't accept your rejection," Dwight added.

"I didn't care for that myself," I said.

"He was just rude and obnoxious and—oooh!" Max, having walked through the wall, stomped her foot. "I didn't like him at all."

"Really?" Grandpa Dave asked. "You hid it well."

She chuckled. "What can I say? I'm a class act."

"You certainly are," he said. "I came to pick up my mask."

"I haven't even had a chance to look at our masks yet," I said.

Zoe took two white boxes from her backpack. There was an elaborate blue *Z* on the top of each box. "What do you think? It's my logo."

"I think it's terrific," I said. "I think you should use it as your logo on everything you produce."

"I'm way ahead of you." She opened the box to reveal the beautiful mask she'd designed for me. She gingerly picked it up out of the box and turned it around so I could see the back. There was the *Z* in the righthand corner.

"Good for you!" I was glad she was personalizing her work.

"Thanks. I hoped you wouldn't be mad. I put it on every mask I've made—well, most of them. I didn't think of it until I'd been making the masks for about a week."

"I knew all along," Max said. "But I didn't say anything because it was Zoe's news to share."

Grandpa Dave opened his mask. "I'll feel as debonaire as Fred Astaire wearing this."

Zoe had no clue who Fred Astaire was, and I could see the wheels turning in Max's head to look him up later.

"But for now, I must be off." He put his mask back in the box. "I'm taking Monica to brunch." He kissed my cheek. "I'm looking forward to escorting you to the ball this evening, Pup."

"Thanks, Grandpa."

"I need to pop out for a while myself," Max said. "I need to conserve my energy so I can be here for the ball this evening."

I wondered if that was truly her intention or if she was going upstairs to spy on Grandpa Dave and Monica. I sorta hoped it was the latter.

Chapter Five

I was straightening up the atelier before going home to get ready for the ball when Monica gave a perfunctory knock and then came in through the door leading into the atelier.

"Hello!" She gave me a bright smile that struck me as being a little too bright. It made me suspicious.

"Hi, Monica. I hope you aren't here for a dress to wear to the ball this evening. The racks are pretty bare at this point."

"Oh, no. Don't worry about that. I'll be staying home this evening eating takeout and researching properties in Nebraska."

"Really?" I folded some unused fabric back onto a bolt and placed it on the shelf. "Have you made up your mind then? I thought you were still on the fence."

Monica ran her fingertips across the tabletop. "Nope. I'm going. My extended visit made me realize how much of my grandchildren's lives I'm missing, and it was wonderful to reconnect with my son."

I frowned slightly. "Reconnect?"

"Well, we were never estranged by any means, but you know how it is when children have families of their own—you become an extension of their family rather than being right at the heart of it." She spread her hands. "Look at you and your parents. You have your own lives now."

"Yes, and I'd say we're richer for it," I said.

She pounced on my words like a fox on a June bug. "Exactly! That's why I want you to encourage Dave to accompany me to Nebraska. It will be good for both of you to put some distance between you. Don't you feel as if you two are smothering each other now?"

"Not at all." I stiffened.

"I know you love your grandfather, Amanda, and he adores you too; but what if you get married and have a family? Then you won't have as much time for him. He'll feel isolated and lonely. You don't want that, do you?"

"Absolutely not, which is why I will *always* have room in my life for Grandpa."

Monica pressed her lips together and shook her head. "You need to think of him now rather than yourself."

"I *am* thinking of him. He needs to be here with his family."

Sighing, Monica turned. "I hoped I could make you see reason. It's obvious you can't." She left the room.

Taking a cue from Max, who was still fortunately absent, I poked a tongue out at her retreating back. "I am not being selfish," I told Jazzy. "*She* is. What if she drags Grandpa Dave off to Nebraska, and they buy a home, and then she dies? He'll be out there with a bunch of strangers. Ugh." I picked the cat up and pressed my face against the top of her head. "We can't let him go."

The questions that went unasked were, *Can I stop him?* and *Should I stop him?* I knew it wasn't my place to make decisions for Grandpa Dave, and I'd support him no matter what. But I desperately hoped he'd stay here in Abingdon.

I took Jazzy home, fed her, and made sure she had everything she needed before I started getting ready. After eating a quick snack of peanut butter crackers, I took a bath.

I sat at the vanity in my white terry robe and put my hair up in an elegant French twist to fully show off the back of my gown. Rhinestone-studded bobby pins added some sparkle.

Dad sent a video chat request as I was applying my makeup.

"Hi, Dad!"

"Hi, Princess. You look gorgeous."

"You know that's right. I'm rocking this robe."

"You are," he said. "I spoke with your grandpa this morning. He seemed excited about the ball."

"What else did he say?" I brushed eyeshadow onto my eyelids.

"He mentioned Monica's offer to accompany her to Nebraska."

I gave a low growl. "Monica paid me a visit before I left work and tried to coerce me into encouraging Grandpa to go with her. She acted like I was being a selfish brat for not wanting him to leave. But what if they get out there and get settled and then she up and dies, Dad? Has anyone thought of that?"

"You clearly have."

"He'd be miserable, that's what." I squinted at my mirror as I applied my eyeliner.

"He could always come back," Dad said. "Whatever he decides doesn't mean it's permanent."

"Maybe not, but it's a loooong way from here to Nebraska—over fourteen hours driving. I looked it up. I don't want to deny Grandpa his happiness. But there are a lot of fish in the sea—this sea! The sea right here in Abingdon!"

"You do realize there is no sea in Abingdon, don't you, Princess?"

I gave him a glare that had him telling me again how pretty I looked. Then he told me to enjoy myself and ended the call.

Parents and grandparents. Good grief. Why couldn't they just do what's best for them—told to them by someone who knows what's best for them?

As Grandpa Dave and I walked into the Brea Ridge Fairgrounds Main Exhibit Hall, I marveled over how hard someone had worked to transform the space into a beautiful venue for the ball. Round tables with seating for four were draped with white tablecloths, and each table contained a centerpiece vase filled with feathers, faux pearls, a mask with a holder, and white mums. Fairy lights were strung across the room and provided most of the lighting.

"Good evening, Tuckers."

Recognizing Jason's voice, I turned and smiled. "Hi, there."

"If you'll step right this way, I'll take your photograph." He ushered us to the photo area where there were two columns of gold, white, and silver balloons topped with feathery white palm fronds on either side of a gold sequined drape.

Jason posed Grandpa and me in the positions he wanted us, returned to his tripod, and snapped two or three photographs. “Now, could you remove the masks for another?”

“Sure.” I carefully maneuvered my mask off my face without messing up my hair. “Why don’t I hear music yet? I thought there was going to be dancing.”

“There’s supposed to be,” Jason said, looking through the camera lens and making some adjustments before taking our photo again.

“Well, they had a last-minute catering change,” Grandpa said. “Maybe their DJ quit too. I’d be up for giving it a go if they need me.”

“Nah, let’s find Zoe and see if she knows what’s going on.” I smiled at Jason. “I’ll see *you* later. I believe you promised me a dance—you never said anything about there having to be music.”

“You’ve got it.”

Grandpa and I zigzagged through the crowd, and I recognized several of the gowns I’d made. Fortunately, we’d put our masks back on and didn’t have to make small talk with anyone while we searched for Zoe.

Even though they were standing around in small groups chatting, no one else seemed to have any more of a clue as to what to do than Grandpa or I did. Maybe Renata Crenshaw was going to give a speech or something to kick off the evening and tell us what we could expect. She should hurry and give the people something exciting. If she didn't, they might begin to leave.

We found Zoe in a far corner of the room. She looked miserable.

"Honey, what's wrong?" I asked, as I hurried to her.

"I got Mom in trouble," she said. "Her boss is an even bigger jerk than his son is apparently."

"The filthy sidewinder asked Maggie why she'd brought her kid to the party," Max said.

Zoe turned her phone around to show us that she was on a video call with Max. The sound had been turned down, so I could barely hear Max; but the fact that she was yelling helped.

"Mom told him he'd asked the servers to bring people to help tonight, and he said *by people I meant hot women, not high school girls*."

"Would you like us to drive you home?" Grandpa asked.

"In a little while," Zoe said. "I'm gonna let Max see more of the outfits first."

"I've seen all I care to see," Max said. "Unless somebody punches that Preston Diggs right in his big, fat schnoz. I'd love to see that!"

A scream pierced the air, and the buzz of conversation stilled. Another scream sliced through the silence.

Some people stood frozen in place. Some hurried in the direction of the screams. Some raced toward the exits.

I moved slightly in front of Zoe to protect her from whatever might happen next and grabbed Grandpa Dave's hand. "Let's just be still. We'll know what's going on anytime now."

"I agree," Grandpa said. "It's best that we stay out of the way, at least, until we get a handle on what's happening."

Seconds later, we heard someone shout, "Call 9-1-1! Preston Diggs has been stabbed!"

Chapter Six

Jason found me and Grandpa Dave standing in the back left corner of the room. Zoe had gone to tell Maggie that we were taking her home.

"Are you all right?" he asked.

"We're fine," I said. "Are you?"

He nodded. "Where's Zoe?"

"She went to talk with her mom," Grandpa said. "I feel like we need to get Zoe out of here as quickly as possible. I realize she's not quite a child anymore, but she isn't as grown up as she'd like to pretend she is either."

"The police have cleared me to leave," Jason said. "I'm going to pack up my equipment, take it home, and check on Rascal. Could I meet you at your place?"

"Sure," I said. "Bring Rascal."

"All right." He gave me a quick kiss. "Be careful."

"You, too."

He nodded at Grandpa and then went to gather his photography gear.

"I like that young man," Grandpa said.

Unable to stop my lips from curling into a smile despite the circumstances, I said, "Thanks. So do I."

I suppressed my smile when I saw Zoe approaching.

"Mom said it's okay for you guys to take me home, but I'm thinking maybe I should stay with her. She seems really upset." She took a steadying breath. "She's the one who found Mr. Diggs with the knife in his chest."

Grandpa and I exchanged quick looks, and he said, "Let me go check on Maggie."

We knew each other well enough to realize we were thinking the same thing—if Maggie found the victim, she was likely the prime suspect in the eyes of the police. Zoe was old and wise enough to come to that conclusion as well, but I wasn't about to point it out if she hadn't connected those dots yet herself.

I put a hand on her shoulder, thinking she suddenly looked terribly young and small.

Grandpa returned to say that Maggie insisted on our taking Zoe home. "She said she'll be home as soon as possible but that it might take a while for the police to interview everyone on the catering staff as well as other people who were near when the incident took place."

"She didn't say she'd rather have me stay with her?" Zoe asked.

"Actually, I think she'd feel better knowing you were home with your papaw," Grandpa said.

"That's true. She didn't much like leaving him home alone this evening. But it *was* supposed to be good money for me before Mr. Diggs blew up and didn't want me here."

I gritted my teeth and refrained from calling Mr. Diggs a jerk. It wasn't nice to speak ill of the dead and all that, but—what a jerk! Rather than comment, I simply led Zoe through the maze of people and out into the crisp air.

Taking a deep breath, I filled my lungs with the fresh scent of pine. The exhibit hall had already begun to feel oppressive, even though many of the guests fled the scene prior to the arrival of the police. Not that it would do them any good—the officers had the guest list.

Other partygoers had stayed merely to see what would happen next, and I supposed there were a few who had remained from a sense of duty. Grandpa and I had done so, more from a sense of responsibility to Zoe than to telling the police what we did or didn't see. We hadn't seen a thing.

When we got to Zoe's house, Dwight was video chatting with Max.

"Max tells me there was some excitement at the masquerade ball," he said.

"There was. Mom's boss was stabbed." Zoe went over to his chair and kissed his stubbly cheek. "She'll be here as soon as she can. She and the rest of the catering staff had to stay because they're all potential witnesses."

The four adults in the room—video, for Max—stared awkwardly at each other. We understood that Maggie was in a precarious position.

"Have you eaten?" Dwight asked.

"No." Zoe dropped her backpack onto the sofa. "They hadn't even started dishing out the food yet. And there wasn't any music either. Even before the murder, it was the worst party ever."

"It was pretty bad," I said.

"Zoe, would you mind cooking us up some burgers?"

I had a feeling Dwight's request was mostly because he wanted to speak with Grandpa and me alone. Maybe I could give him a chance to speak with Grandpa. "I need to get home and change clothes soon, but before I do that, Zoe and I could go get something."

"No need. I don't mind cooking," Zoe said. "I like to fry burgers."

"All right," I said.

"Thanks, Dimples." Dwight smiled. "Are you sure you two won't reconsider? She makes better burgers than her mother does." He turned to Zoe. "Don't tell her I said that!"

Grinning, she picked up her backpack and went up the stairs. "I'll put my stuff up and be right back."

Dwight's smile quickly faded as soon as Zoe left the room. Once he was satisfied that she was in her room, he lowered his voice and asked, "How bad could this be for Maggie?"

"Hard to say," Grandpa said. "All we know right now is that Maggie found the body."

"Jason was still at the exhibit hall packing up his photography equipment when we left." I glanced over my shoulder to make sure Zoe wasn't coming back yet or standing at the top of the stairs eavesdropping. I'd done my fair share of that when I was her age. "Hopefully, he'll be able to tell us more about what was going on since he was around more people than we were at the time. We'd just found Zoe when everything went crazy."

Grandpa patted Dwight's shoulder. "Call us if you need anything."

I climbed the stairs to give Zoe a quick hug and to tell her goodnight.

"Everything will be all right," she said. "Won't it?"

"Sure, it will." I hoped I wasn't lying to her.

In the living room, Dwight was no longer chatting with Max. On the way to my house, Grandpa told me she'd said she needed to refresh her energy in case she was needed later.

"Also, I invited Dwight, Zoe, and Maggie to Sunday lunch," he said.

"That's good." I sighed.

"I hope so too, Pup."

"Hope what?" I asked.

"That Maggie isn't in jail awaiting arraignment."

Grandpa Dave helped me unfasten the buttons at the back of my gown and ordered a pizza while I went to change into jeans and a sweatshirt. When I returned, he'd hung up his suit jacket, removed his tie, and rolled up his sleeves.

"There are some of Dad's old clothes still in his closet if you'd like to change out of your dress clothes," I said.

"I'm all right. I appreciate the offer, though."

Jason and the pizza arrived at almost the same time. Rascal, or a white blur I thought was Rascal, whizzed past all of us into the house. He did zoomies around the kitchen and living room, ran back outside, did a lap around the yard, and finally came to a stop in the living room where he stood looking up at me with his tongue lolled out the side of his mouth.

"We'd better get you a drink of water." I led the dog into the kitchen, took out the silver bowl I used for his water, and filled it with water from the fridge.

As Jason and Grandpa Dave got out plates and napkins, I opened the treat jar and got something for Rascal.

Jazzy came into the kitchen to give the dog the onceover. When he finished lapping his water, he shook his head, spattering water on her from his whiskers. She flicked her tail. They treated each other with icy politeness—not quite friends yet, but they would hopefully get there one of these days.

We sat down at the kitchen table to enjoy our pizza and soft drinks, no one quite wanting to broach the subject of Preston Diggs yet.

When I could no longer stand the suspense, I asked Jason, "Do you know if anyone was arrested before you left?"

"Not as far as I know. The police allowed me to leave because I was taking photos at the time and the couple and I could vouch for each other's whereabouts. Plus, my camera has a digital readout telling exactly when each photograph is taken."

"Is there any way Mr. Diggs's death could have been an accident?" I felt like it was a dumb question as soon as it was out of my mouth, but I was hoping. "I mean, everyone was rushing around in that area they'd partitioned off for the food preparation area…"

Grandpa shook his head. "The stabbing was deliberate—too accurate to have been anything but murder."

"I know the police has everyone's name and number, but who besides the catering staff was either asked to stay by the deputies or volunteered to remain at the exhibit hall?" I asked.

Jason wiped his mouth with his napkin. "Renata Crenshaw was running around clucking like a broody hen off her nest. She appeared to be more upset that her party had been ruined than that Preston Diggs was dead."

I told Jason about Preston Diggs's reaction to Maggie bringing her to the ball. "He'd asked the servers to bring extra helpers, but apparently, he'd wanted them to be hot women rather than kids."

"Yeah, um…" Jason sighed. "I overheard someone saying they heard Maggie shouting at Mr. Diggs a few minutes prior to the scream."

"I'm sure she was giving him a dressing down over the way he'd treated Zoe," Grandpa said. "And I don't blame her. I'm surprised she didn't quit then and there."

"The only reason I can think of that she didn't was because she didn't want to bail on the other servers," I said.

"So, Jason, when you left, who else did you notice was still there?" Grandpa took a drink of his soda.

"Mr. Diggs's son, of course."

"Did he appear to be upset?" I asked. "I don't really know the man, but family is always under a microscope when someone is murdered."

"I couldn't say." Jason polished off one slice of pizza and grabbed another.

We ate in silence for a few minutes, and then there was a frantic knocking on the door.

"It's me—Maggie!"

I hurried to the living room and opened the door.

Maggie came into the room and burst into tears. "I don't know what to do. The police think I killed Preston Diggs."

Chapter Seven

Grandpa Dave gave Maggie one of his famous bear hugs until she could get her sobs under control. Then he led her into the kitchen and asked, "Exactly why do the police believe you're guilty of stabbing Mr. Diggs, other than the fact that you found him?"

"He and I argued only a few minutes before I found him. That pretty much clenched it." Maggie took a seat at the table. "After they finished questioning me, even I was beginning to think I was guilty. I'm not, though, I promise."

"Do you have any idea who might actually be guilty?" I asked.

"I have no idea," she said.

"Just think a minute." Jason patted Rascal's head. The dog had sensed the tension in the room and had come to sit by Jason's chair. "Who did you see with or around Mr. Diggs prior to the murder?"

"All the staff of Hot Diggity was there, of course. He'd closed the restaurant for the night because he made so much off the masquerade ball, and it was also really good publicity for the restaurant." She shook her head. "Sorry, my mind's all jumbled up right now. Anyway, Ms. Crenshaw was there, Tony Diggs, a few people from the historical society… Two were there asking about the food—one was allergic to shellfish, and the other was asking if there was any alcohol in any of the dishes."

"You don't know the names of the people from the historical society?" Grandpa asked.

"No, but I also recall someone reporting to Ms. Crenshaw that the DJ had been in a fender bender on his way to the event and would be late if he made it at all," she said. "The guy was frantic because he didn't know what they'd do if there was no music."

"That's one of the first things I noticed when we walked into the exhibit hall," I said. "No music."

"Ms. Crenshaw made an announcement asking if anyone on the catering staff had any DJ experience, but the DJ had his equipment in his vehicle. I'm not sure what she was thinking—I believe she was merely grasping at straws."

"Poor Ms. Crenshaw. Everything about this party began falling apart before it even began." I quickly realized I'd put the party above Mr. Diggs's death. "I mean, not to belittle what happened to Mr. Diggs in the least, but…"

"I understand what you're saying," Maggie said, with a slight smile. "Mr. Diggs certainly didn't appreciate her trying to hijack a member of his staff and told Ms. Crenshaw he needed every person he'd hired for the evening and could use more. To which *she* replied that he wouldn't need any of his staff if the guests left because they couldn't dance."

"A valid point," Jason said. "People were getting awfully restless."

"Ms. Crenshaw also reminded Mr. Diggs that she was not only paying his fee but that she was doing him and his overhyped—her exact words," Maggie said, "—restaurant a favor by even allowing him to be there. I was glad she put him in his place because it made me realize I wasn't the only one feeling like this guy was a creep. I left a decent job to go work for him, and I was going to quit after tonight."

"Where were you when the stabbing occurred?" Grandpa asked.

"I'd gone over to help with the charcuterie boards. There was to be one placed on each table. Mr. Diggs called to me, and I shouted back that I'd be there in just a second because I wanted to make sure the board I was preparing was correctly done and ready to be served before I walked away." She took a napkin from the holder in the center of the table and dabbed at her eyes and nose. "He told me to hurry it up and said, 'It's about your kid!' Well, that made me lose my temper."

"I can imagine," I murmured.

"I stormed back to where he'd been standing, and there he lay." She took a steadying breath. "I screamed twice, unable at first to believe what I was seeing. Another member of the catering staff must've called 9-1-1, but I instinctively knew Mr. Diggs had died already. I'll never forget those staring, unblinking eyes."

"It appears to me that all the evidence against you is hearsay." Grandpa got up from the table, got a glass, filled it with water, and placed it in front of Maggie. "You argued with the man, but so did Renata Crenshaw. He called for you to come talk with him, and when you arrived, he was lying on the floor with a knife in his chest. Am I correct in thinking all the catering staff were wearing gloves?"

"We were." With a trembling hand, Maggie raised the glass of water to her lips.

Feeling bad that I hadn't thought to offer the woman something to drink myself, I asked, "Would you like something to eat, Maggie?"

"No, thanks." She sat the glass back down.

"Has anyone come forward as an eyewitness?" Jason asked.

"Not as far as I know," Maggie said. "Although how there could be that many people milling around and nobody see what happened is beyond me." After drinking the rest of the water, Maggie announced that she needed to get home. "I'm sure Zoe and Daddy are worried."

"I need to be shuffling off myself." Grandpa stood. "Do you need me to drive you home?"

"No. I'll be fine." Maggie pushed back her chair and rose to her feet. "Thank you all for everything."

"You, Zoe, and Dwight should join us for lunch tomorrow at my house," Grandpa said. "Jason, you, too."

"I'd love to, Dave, but unfortunately, I have an appointment for a family portrait."

Jason and I walked Grandpa and Maggie to the door and told them goodnight. I wandered back into the kitchen and put the dishes into the dishwasher as Jason tidied up the table.

After tearing down the pizza box and putting it in the trash, he slipped his arms around my waist. "Did I tell you how beautiful you look tonight?"

"So did you—so *do* you," I corrected. "Ugh. I'm sorry tonight was such a disaster. I mean, I hate that Mr. Diggs got killed, and I hope Maggie doesn't get arrested—what a nightmare that would be for their family—but I'm also sad for the Brea Ridge Historical

Society. They put so much work into the masquerade ball, spent all that time and money on the event, and then had it ruined before it had even begun."

"I know. I didn't even get that dance I'd been looking forward to for days."

Smiling, I said, "That, I can fix."

I took out my phone, opened my music app, and put on a romantic songs playlist. After placing the phone on the table, I walked back into Jason's waiting arms. As we danced, and avoided stumbling over Rascal, I tried to push the evening's concerns out of my mind; but I couldn't help but be afraid of what tomorrow might bring.

After Jason and Rascal left, I sank onto the living room sofa and opened the social media app on my phone. I was hoping to speak with Max. Judging by the message box, it didn't appear she was online, but I sent her a message anyway.

Moments later, my phone buzzed, and I had a video chat request from myself, which I knew to be Max on my old tablet. I accepted the invitation, and Max's image filled the screen. Although the lights were off in the shop, the moon was bright, and I could see her clearly. She was in the reception area next to the desk, and her eyes were filled with concern.

"How are Zoe and Dwight?" I asked.

"More nervous than a long-tailed cat at the rocking chair warehouse."

"Did you get to talk with either of them after Maggie got home?"

"No. When they heard her coming, we ended our call. You know how she feels about me."

Inclining my head, I said, "I know how she feels about me too, but this is where she came when she was allowed to leave the exhibit hall."

Her eyes widened. "Are you jiving me?"

I took *jiving* to mean kidding. "I promise I'm not." I told her about Maggie's visit.

"The poor duck must be half-scared out of her mind," Max said.

"She told us there were members of the historical society hanging around, but she didn't know their names. Maybe Ruby Mills can help us figure out who they were."

Ruby had been one of my first clients when I opened Designs on You, and she was also a member of the historical society.

"I simply cannot comprehend how there were so many people present, and not one of them saw this man get stabbed." She raised her thumbnail to her mouth. "It's almost as if no one *wanted* to see anything."

"Or they didn't realize what was happening. Maggie told us Mr. Diggs was already dead when she got to him—she could tell by his lifeless eyes." I grabbed my tablet off the coffee table and typed *instant death by stabbing* into the search bar. "He should've shouted, fought off his attacker, done *something*."

"What are you looking for?" Max asked.

"I'm not convinced Preston Diggs was stabbed to death. What if he died and was then stabbed to throw investigators off track?"

"Darling, I appreciate your mental gymnastics, I really do. But don't you think you're stretching a bit far on this one?"

"I might be, but work with me here. What if Mr. Diggs was poisoned? His killer, being at the masquerade ball in the midst of all the behind-the-scenes chaos, sees that the poison has taken effect and that Mr. Diggs is about to die. Not wanting an autopsy to show poison in his victim's system, the killer stabs Mr. Diggs to create an obvious cause of death for the police."

"But where did this person go?" Max asked. "He or she was bound to have blood on their clothing or on their hands at the very least."

"Not necessarily. They might've been wearing gloves, and the wound might not have bled as long as the knife was in place."

"All right then. Where are the bloody gloves?"

"I don't know." I expelled a long breath. "I guess I really am reaching."

"No, kiddo, you're asking some important questions."

"I might be asking," I said, "but I don't have the faintest idea of where to begin finding the answers."

Chapter Eight

On Sunday morning while I was having toast and coffee at the kitchen table, I called Dad. I hoped I was correct in assuming that Mom wasn't awake yet. While Dad had always been an early riser, Mom had been a night owl.

"Good morning, Princess."

Given the fact that he was speaking in a hushed tone, I thought I must be right. "Hi. Is Mom still in bed?"

"She is."

"Okay, please don't say anything to her about this because she'd have a fit and want to know why I don't just mind my own business and let the police do their jobs."

"Another murder, huh?"

"Yeah." I crunched into my toast.

"I won't say anything about it for now, but tell me what's going on."

Between bites of toast and sips of coffee, I explained to him how the masquerade ball got cut terribly short when the caterer, Preston Diggs, was murdered.

"Preston Diggs? Hmm…that name sounds familiar. Did his kid have a crush on you at one time?"

"Yes." *Should I tell him he still does? Nah—not relevant.* "And he was at the ball when his dad was killed."

"Is he a suspect?"

"Maybe. The *main* suspect right now is Maggie, Zoe's mom."

"Yikes. What evidence do they have?"

"Not much," I said. "The main thing is that she found the body, but he called to her a couple minutes prior to that. She came by here last night when the police finished with her—"

"Really? Wow."

"I know. She didn't want to go home and face Zoe and Dwight yet, and—" I sighed. "Other than her family, we must be all she's got."

"I'm glad she has you and Dad. You're a fantastic pair to be on anyone's team."

"Well, speaking of being a team, have you told Mom that Grandpa is thinking about moving to Nebraska?"

"I have." Dad was being reticent.

"And what was her opinion about that?"

"She said your grandpa is a grown man and that he has to do what's right for him."

"Uh-huh. Is that *your* opinion too?" I asked.

"Kind of. I mean, yeah, I guess it is. I like that Dad's there with you—that the two of you have each other—especially since your mother and I are so far away from you now. But we have to let your grandpa make up his own mind."

"Yeah, well, we don't have to like it. By the way, Monica came into Designs on You yesterday and asked me to try to persuade Grandpa to go with her! As if *that* will ever happen!" I emitted a low growl before biting into my toast with a vengeance.

"Sweetheart, the best thing you can do is let Grandpa make his own decision," he said softly. "That way, there won't be any resentments at the end of the day."

"What? You think I'd guilt Grandpa into staying?"

"I'm not saying that at all." He sighed, apparently aware that he was making a mess of it. "I'm only saying that whenever we tried to persuade you to do anything, you'd do the exact opposite."

"I know. But Monica talked as if I'd be relieved to have Grandpa out of my everyday life, and that infuriated me."

"It would have made me angry too. But it'll all work out, Princess, I promise." In the background, I heard Mom come into the room and ask what would work out. "Dad's situation with Monica."

"Tell her to worry about her own life," Mom said loud enough for me to hear, "and let Dave manage his own."

"I heard," I told Dad. "I'll talk with you later."

At around eleven a.m., I put Jazzy into her carrier and the carrier into the back seat of my car and headed to Grandpa's house. Grandpa lived on the outskirts of Abingdon in a more rural area of town. I'd always loved his house—the wraparound front porch with the rocking chairs and swing, the spectacular view, all the wonderful times I'd had there with Grandpa Dave and Grandma Jodie before she passed a few years ago.

I shook off my melancholy as I pulled into the driveway and parked the car. Getting out, I opened the back door and unlatched the gate to Jazzy's carrier. There was no need to worry about her getting hit by a car here—we were too far from the road, and she loved Grandpa and his house so much that she always ran to the porch as fast as she could go and turned around to see what was keeping me.

The smell of beef, potatoes, onions, and cornbread greeted me when I walked through the door.

"Hi, Grandpa! You must've started lunch without me because it smells wonderful!"

"I did." He came out of the kitchen wiping his hands on a dish towel. "I have beef stew in the slow cooker, and there's a pan of cornbread ready to go into the oven." He kissed my cheek. "I didn't want us to have to cook when you got here."

"But that's half the fun."

He chuckled. "All right then. You can help me with the salad."

As we shredded lettuce and diced vegetables, I told him I thought we should ask Max to join us.

"I know Maggie isn't comfortable around Max, but right now she needs all the help she can get. Besides, Max is almost always with us for at least part of Sunday lunch."

"I agree," he said. "Maybe Maggie will feel more at ease with Max on a screen rather than face to face."

"I don't know. Zoe has tried to encourage Maggie to video chat with Max before, but Maggie refuses."

"This is different, Pup. Maggie came to your house last night. That surprised me. I believe she realizes she needs people she can count on." He sighed. "Especially if this investigation goes badly for her."

I opened my mouth to tell him my crazy theory about poison as the primary method of murder, but the doorbell rang. I figured that was probably for the best. I could tell the entire group over lunch. And Max could help me.

As Grandpa opened the door, I sent a video chat request to Max. She accepted.

"Hiya. What do we know today?"

"Dwight, Zoe, and Maggie just arrived at Grandpa's for lunch, and I'm having you join us. I'll put you on the buffet like I usually do, so you can see everyone at the table."

"And they can see me," she said. "Is everybody all right with that?"

"They should be. You're all guests of Grandpa Dave."

"We'll see."

I carried the phone into the dining room and placed it on the buffet facing the table. "Be right back."

"I'll be here with—well, with this garb I died wearing on."

Unable to suppress a laugh, I said, "Well, you look gorgeous."

"I know that, darling, but it would be nice to change things up once in a while."

In the living room, Grandpa was telling Dwight, Zoe, and Maggie that the cornbread should be ready any minute and that we could eat.

"Shall we go on into the dining room?" I asked. "Max is already there waiting for us."

Maggie looked slightly uncomfortable, but she didn't say anything. Zoe ran on ahead to speak with Aunt Max, and Dwight merely gave me a surreptitious wink.

When we all, except Max, had our food and drinks in front of us, we mainly ate in awkward silence for a minute or two. Then Grandpa Dave mentioned how pretty the weather had been lately, and Dwight complimented him on the food, and then I couldn't take it anymore.

Taking a drink of tea to clear my throat and steady my nerves, I said, "Max and I were talking last night about how odd it was that Mr. Diggs didn't shout or create any kind of scene at all when he was attacked."

"The investigating officers commented on that as well," Maggie said. "One thought it could be because the killer was so precise that Mr. Diggs died almost as soon as the knife pierced him. The other wasn't so sure."

"I'm in the unsure officer's camp," I said. "What if Mr. Diggs was poisoned and then stabbed as he was about to die?"

"That makes no sense." Maggie looked around at the other faces at the table to see if anyone else thought my theory was feasible. "Why would anyone double-kill the man?"

Max decided it was time to toss in her two pennies. "I found it a tough mouthful to swallow myself until Amanda gave me a reason to chew it over some more.

She said the stabbing might've been intended to throw the coppers off the scent of the real killer."

"Right." I picked up the thread again. "Let's say the killer poisoned Mr. Diggs but wanted to set himself or herself above suspicion. What better way than to stab him in a crowd as he was going down?"

"The killer's timing would have had to have been perfect, and the killer would have had to have had the sleight of hand ability of a skilled magician," Grandpa Dave said.

"True, but the killer would have also needed a great deal of skill or luck to kill him without his making any noise," Dwight said.

"While I agree with the theory that it *could've* worked the way Amanda says, Mr. Diggs wasn't even supposed to be catering the event until the day before," Zoe reminded us all. "He was a last-minute replacement for the other catering company."

"Sure, but what if the killer had planned for Diggs to die at his fancy new restaurant?" Max asked. "Maybe the poison had been administered prior to the event, and the killer got fed up with waiting for the palooka to die and just stuck him already?"

"What difference does any of it make?" Maggie asked. "The police know the man was stabbed, and they think I did it."

"We're simply trying to come up with an alternate scenario," Dwight said softly, placing his left hand on his daughter's arm.

"I know, and I appreciate that. But right now my brain feels fried, and I'd like to enjoy this delicious meal while talking about something—anything—else."

"I'm making a D in algebra," Zoe said.

"Do you need a tutor, Dimples?" Dwight asked.

"No." She puffed out her cheeks. "I lied. I'm averaging a B. I was being dramatic to start a new conversation."

Max laughed. "A young woman with Englebright blood in her veins being dramatic?" She pressed her hand to her chest. "I can hardly believe it!"

Dwight gestured toward Maggie. "You should've seen this one when she was told she couldn't dye her hair. She tried to do it herself with orange drink mix powder."

Covering her mouth with her napkin as she chortled, Maggie said, "It was such a mess! It was the color of fake cheese, but only in patches."

"Oh, it was awful." Dwight shook his head. "Her mother immediately took her to the sink and started scrubbing the child's head."

"I was afraid I'd be bald when she got through with me," Maggie said. "And I *still* had cheddar-tinged hair for two weeks."

"Wow. No wonder you took me to a salon when I said I wanted blue hair," Zoe said.

Maggie nodded at her daughter. "I'd already been there and done that. I didn't want you to try to do it yourself." She turned and looked at the screen, surprising the rest of us. "What about you, Aunt Max? Do you have any hair disaster stories?"

A broad smile spread over Max's face. "Well, let me tell you about the first time I got my hair cut."

Chapter Nine

After lunch, I helped Grandpa Dave clean up, and then I left. I usually stayed for a while on Sunday afternoons, but he seemed out of sorts today. I told him I'd be at home if he'd like to watch a movie later.

"Aw, now, I imagine your young man will be coming over," he said.

"I'm not sure. We haven't made plans." I thought maybe Monica was coming over or that he was going to her house, but I didn't mention it. I imagined her showing him photographs of beautiful homes in Nebraska that could be theirs. The very idea made my beef stew lie heavily on my stomach.

I took a container of leftover beef stew with me, and I decided to swing by Shops on Main and put it into the refrigerator for tomorrow's lunch. When I got there, however, I saw Jason's jeep and a minivan in the parking lot.

Putting all four windows down so Jazzy would remain cool in her carrier, I took my keys, purse, and container of beef stew and went to the back door. It was unlocked, so I went on inside and straight to the kitchen.

My intention was to put the beef stew in the fridge, and then say a quick hello to Max before going upstairs to greet Jason and the family he was photographing. The plan was going well. I opened the refrigerator, put the beef stew on the bottom shelf, closed the door, and then I saw a white, furry blur leap off the top of the refrigerator and onto my head.

Uttering a squeal of alarm, I hopped backward, shaking my head, as the creature ran down my side. It stopped at my waist for good measure.

Max appeared, saw what was happening, and yelled, "Shoo, weasel, shoo!"

The animal sprinted down my leg and out of the kitchen.

Weasel. Ferret. Joey Conrad. Biscuit.

"Oh, shucks. The Conrads are probably looking all over for that thing." I clucked my tongue. "Come here, Biscuit. Come back."

But it was frightened, and I had no idea where it had gone. The shops were all closed, so that was one good thing.

"Sorry," Max said. "I knew Jason was here and that he had clients upstairs, but I hadn't realized they were the Conrads. If I'd known, I'd have kept myself hidden. You know those weasels scare me."

We at Shops on Main had quite a history with Joey Conrad and his ferrets, Biscuit and Gravy. It all started when they got loose in Designs on You. Then they went down a girl's shirt during a rehearsal for *Beauty and the Beast* at Winter Garden High School when Joey was playing the part of Chip, the teacup. They ran amok in Shops on Main again around Christmas, and they wreaked some havoc in another shop in Abingdon most recently. They hadn't, as far as I knew, made much mischief around here lately. Well, until now.

Like Jazzy, other animals could see and were fascinated by Max. And while Max loved Jazzy to pieces, she had no affection whatsoever for Joey's "weasels."

"Would you help me corral Biscuit while I go up and get Joey?"

She blew out a breath. "I'll see if I can find the blasted thing."

I hurried upstairs to Jason's studio. Everyone was looking for Biscuit. Under chairs, behind props, in the trash can. Everyone, that is, except Joey. He was standing there looking adorable in a suit and tie while holding Gravy, his brown ferret.

"I'm telling ya, Biscuit will be back in a minute," he said.

"Joey, why in the world did you bring Biscuit and Gravy to the portrait studio?" his mom asked.

"Cuz you said it was a family picture, and they're family!"

I cleared my throat, and everyone turned in my direction.

"Hi, Miss Amanda," Joey said.

"Did you find Biscuit?" his mom asked.

I nodded. "Biscuit is downstairs, and I inadvertently frightened the poor thing after it jumped from the top of the refrigerator and landed on my head."

Joey guffawed. "Biscuit loves to play sneak attack." He handed Gravy to his mom, and said, "Let's go, Miss Amanda."

With a smile over my shoulder at Jason, I followed Joey down the stairs. At the foot of the staircase was Max. Biscuit was standing near her tilting its head first one way and then the other.

"I got killed falling down this stupid flight of stairs," Max told it. "Broke my neck. You should be more careful about not scaring people. Not that I fell because a weasel scared me, but still—you know, it's the principle of the thing."

The ferret skittered sideways, still watching Max intently.

"You owe me," Max said to me.

"Thank you," I said. "I'll get you a new book."

"A new book? Cool," Joey said. "Thanks, Miss Amanda."

Of course, Joey thought I'd been speaking to him because he couldn't hear or see Max. So now I'd have to download a new book to Max's tablet *and* buy a book for Joey.

"Yes." I glared at Max. "The next time you're here, we'll go to Antiquated Editions and get you a book to…to celebrate the start of the new school year."

He shrugged. "Okay. C'mon, Biscuit. Mom is about to blow a gasket over these pictures, so I guess we'd better get up there and try to be on our best behavior." He held the ferret up to his face. "Can you smile?"

The animal's expression didn't change.

"Great, Biscuit! That's perfect!" Joey kissed it on the head.

I went back up to the studio with them to watch the photo shoot and to help catch ferrets, if necessary.

"I'll see you later," Max said.

I wisely didn't respond to her this time.

Watching Jason pose the family—especially Joey and his ferrets—so painstakingly made me appreciate anew how very good he was at his profession. It was obvious that he loved every minute of it. Well, maybe not when Gravy nipped his finger, but the rest of it.

When the photo shoot concluded, Sarah, Joey's mom, came over to me. "I heard about what happened at the masquerade ball. What a shame all those gorgeous gowns you made didn't get to be enjoyed for very long."

"Well, I'm sure they can be worn to another function," I said, with a smile.

"Yeah, the ball." She gave a bark of laughter. "Renata is already reorganizing the masquerade ball, so everyone will have the opportunity to show off your handiwork very soon."

"Huh, I didn't realize that. I'm glad Mr. Diggs's death didn't completely derail their fundraising efforts then."

"I can't imagine the historical society would be happy about returning everyone's money from ticket sales. And the silent auction didn't even get off the ground. I mean, I'm sorry about Mr. Diggs, but it's good that Renata will be able to put it back together within the next couple of weeks."

"Are you good friends with Renata?" I asked.

"Not really. She's a friend of a friend, that sort of thing."

"Oh. I just wondered what happened to the original caterer."

"She fired them," Sarah said. "And between you and me, I wouldn't agree to do the ball again after she'd treated me that way."

"But why did she fire them? Didn't she have a good reason?"

"I have no idea, but I do know Mr. Diggs catered the affair for free and even absorbed the cost of the food."

"Why would he do that?"

Shrugging, she said, "Maybe because Hot Diggity was so new. But the restaurant seemed to be doing well, so I—" She broke off. "Joey, don't you dare let them get down!"

I wanted to hear the rest of her thoughts on why Preston Diggs would incur such a debt. I didn't know the man personally, but I couldn't recall ever hearing the words *Preston Diggs* and *philanthropist* tossed around in the same sentence.

Unfortunately, by the time Sarah and her husband had gotten the children and the ferrets rounded up and on their way to the minivan, she'd completely lost her train of thought. She waved goodbye to me and called out that she'd see me soon.

When they left, Jason let his mask slip. He looked exhausted.

"I brought some beef stew," I said. "Would you like me to go downstairs and heat it up for you?"

"I'd love that. You're an angel."

I slowly descended the stairs, and Max came to join me.

"Did you hear what Sarah Conrad said?" I asked.

"I did. I was listening from the other side of the wall so as not to spook the weasels. Why on earth would a man who'd just invested whatever it costs to open a new restaurant—I'm guessing it's a lot of dough—volunteer to cater a big to-do for free?"

"I don't know. But I intend to find out."

Chapter Ten

As Jason sat in the kitchen eating his stew, I sat across from him and told him about Monica coming to talk with me yesterday morning.

"She really asked me if I'd help persuade Grandpa to move with her to Nebraska! Can you believe that?"

His mouth too full to speak, he nodded.

"What would you do if your grandmother was considering moving to another part of the country?" I asked.

After swallowing and wiping his mouth on his napkin, he said, "I'd say, 'Granny, don't do anything rash. Go to Nebraska for a week or two if you want to, but don't sell out and move. Don't make any snap decisions and do something you'll regret.'"

Max, who'd apparently been listening from somewhere behind me, said, "That's really good advice."

Distracted, I said, "It is." Realizing my faux pas, I added, "Really good advice, Jason."

He laughed. "You don't have to sound so surprised."

"I'm sorry. It wasn't that I was surprised, it's just that you made such an excellent point. He doesn't have to outright move. He doesn't have to get married. He doesn't have to rush into anything."

"Exactly." He took a drink of his soda. "I do have a confession to make, though. That was the advice Granny always gave me when I was trying to make a tough decision."

"She's a clever woman," I said. "Would you like to come over now that you're finished with the Conrads?"

"I have a little more work I need to finish first, but I'd love to see you afterward."

"It's a date."

Jason went back upstairs, and I went into Designs on You and got my old—now Max's tablet.

"What book would you like?" I asked her as she passed through the wall and perched on the worktable.

"I want to read that Victoria Holt novel you were telling me about—*Bride of Pendorric*." She tilted her head. "Maybe I should get Zoe to read it too. And you could read it again, and we could have a little book club to take our minds off our troubles."

"That's not a bad idea." I downloaded the book for Max and gifted a copy of it to Zoe.

I took Jazzy home and tried to relax in front of the television. The cat was curled up on my lap, and there was a sitcom on the screen, but I wasn't really paying attention to what was going on.

My phone rang. It was Zoe.

Muting the TV, I answered the call. "Hey, there."

"Hi. Thanks for the book. Max told me about the book club."

"You're welcome. *Bride of Pendorric* is a book I read years ago and remembered as being really good. I think you'll like it. I plan on rereading it too."

"Aunt Max said we all have a lot on our minds right now and that this will be a good distraction. She told me about Dave. Don't worry. He won't leave."

"How can you be so sure?" I asked.

"He's a good guy who adores his family."

"My dad is a good guy, and he and Mom moved to Florida."

"That's different," she said. "He had to go where his job took him. Dave is too smart to let some pushy tomato make a puppet out of him. He pulls his own strings."

"A pushy tomato, huh?" I laughed.

"I know I'm doing it again—talking like a flapper who died in the 1930s. It gets me some super weird looks at school, but I like talking like Max to you and Papaw and Dave."

"I like it too. And I'm so happy your mom talked with Max today!"

"Right? To be honest, it shocked the heck out of me, but I tried not to act like it was a big deal to Mom."

"I was surprised, too, and I hope it leads to more communication between the two of them in the future."

"I do, too," Zoe said. "But we can't push it. Mom has to get to know Max on her own terms."

"Has your mom said anything about where she might look for a job next? Of course, I'm going on the assumption that Hot Diggity will be closing or sold."

"Tony Diggs called Mom a little while after we got back from lunch with you and Dave. He said he was going to close the restaurant for a few days. I mean, I only heard Mom's side of the conversation, but it sounded like Hot Diggity needed to open back up because they have debts and stuff."

"Then how in the world was Preston Diggs able to comp the historical society for the catering?" I wondered aloud.

"Wait, what?"

I relayed to her the information Sarah Conrad had passed along to me.

"That's the first I've heard of that," she said. "I'd bet Mom doesn't know it either. She probably wouldn't have taken me along if she'd have had any indication I wouldn't get paid for helping."

"That's right. He had the servers all bring someone with them, and I don't imagine they were willing to work for free."

"No, he was going to pay us. Of course, I turned out to be—well, not what he was looking for."

"He was a jerk," I said. "Sarah said he even paid for the food, and I took it that he wasn't getting reimbursed for it either. I understood that he was doing the catering completely free for the historical society."

"That's crazy. Maybe I misunderstood about the restaurant being in the red. Like I said, I only heard Mom's side of the conversation, and Mr. Diggs would have to be super rich to be able to give all that food away and pay his workers and everything. Right?"

"I don't know about super rich, but I certainly wouldn't expect a new restaurant trying to get off the ground to throw away—or maybe *donate* would be the better word—that much money to them. Sure, he could write it off as a business expense, but that's still crazy," I said. "I've been open for over a year, and there's no way I could afford to donate even half the gowns I made for the ball. I could possibly give one as some sort of silent auction item or something, but even that would pinch my pocketbook."

"Pinch your pocketbook?" Zoe laughed. "Nice to know I'm not the only one who talks like Aunt Max sometimes."

"The worst thing is when she makes you sound like a nutcase by talking while someone who doesn't know she's there is in the room, and you answer her!"

"That's true." She paused. "If I get a chance to talk with Mom without it seeming forced, I'll ask her if Mr. Diggs was really doing the catering for free."

"Thanks, Zoe. I appreciate that."

I was determined to get out of the funk I'd been in and not bring my date with Jason down into the dumps. Knowing that bowl of stew wouldn't tide him over for long, I made a pan of brownies. Then when it was closer to time for him to arrive, I prepared a homemade pepperoni and Canadian bacon pizza with mozzarella and cheddar cheeses. I also put bowls of popcorn, pretzels, and peanuts onto the kitchen table, thinking I'd move them into the living room if Rascal didn't come with Jason. And then for the *piece de resistance*, I turned the television onto the football game.

When Jason arrived, his eyes went wide, and his jaw dropped. "Your house smells heavenly, and you're watching the game?"

"I haven't been. I've been busy in the kitchen. You can put it on whatever game you'd like to see."

"This is the game I've wanted to see for a week." He gave me a quick kiss. "What did I do to deserve this?"

"I knew you were giving up the game to come see me. I didn't want you to have to do that."

After kissing me again, he said, "You're the best."

Later as I snuggled against Jason, my stomach full of pizza and brownies, I sincerely hoped that Monica wasn't as smart a tomato as me.

Chapter Eleven

On Monday morning, I did an inventory of my *prete-a-porter*, or ready-to-wear, line. I was out of my popular 1950s-inspired A-line dresses in almost every size and fabric. They were popular year-round. I had a surplus of shorts and halter sets I'd made using a pattern from the 1940s as well as shirtwaist dresses.

I put the shorts sets and dresses onto a rack with a half-price sign attached to the top. Then I pulled my easel into the hall and placed a *SALE* poster on it. I'd had to hurry with the easel because Max wasn't around, and I was afraid Jazzy would run out the door. I needn't have worried, she was already dozing on her bed in the atelier.

Taking out my laptop, I ordered fabric for the A-line dresses. Since I wasn't working on any custom pieces at the moment, I had to decide how to best spend my time. I chose calling loyal clients to let them know I was having a sale. The first person I called was Ruby Mills.

Ruby answered my call on the first ring. “Hello, dear. How are you holding up? I thought it was absolutely dreadful that the masquerade ball turned into such a disaster. That was supposed to be your night to shine.”

Chuckling, I said, “I appreciate the sentiment, but I believe the historical society was supposed to be in the spotlight.”

“Well, of course, but you took such pains making those beautiful gowns. I told Renata the least she could do would be to give you tickets to the ball so you could see all your beautiful creations in the wild.”

So that’s why Renata offered the tickets at the last minute.

“I appreciate that, Ruby. I understand that rescheduling the event is already underway.”

“It is indeed.”

“You know, I heard a rumor that Mr. Diggs volunteered his catering services, including the food. That was awfully generous of him.”

“Well, now, he didn’t exactly do it out of the goodness of his heart.” Ruby went on to explain that Preston Diggs had caused the other caterer to be fired. “He sent Renata an email telling her that the caterer they’d hired had caused an outbreak of food poisoning at a wedding he attended. Renata passed that information along in a newsletter to the historical society and announced that Mr. Diggs would be catering the event."

"But that doesn't explain why he did it for free," I said.

"I'm getting to that part. The caterer found out about the newsletter and threatened to sue everyone involved for libel. Her daddy is a lawyer, so he was ready to get the ball rolling. To keep that from happening, the historical society had to pay the caterer's fee."

"And Mr. Diggs?"

"Well, since he was the match that lit the fire, he had to cater the event for nothing." Ruby laughed. "That had been his intention all along—to get the other caterer fired so he could do it himself. But he thought he'd be paid handsomely for it. He botched that up, didn't he?"

"He certainly did. It sounds as if he got what he deserved." Realizing how harsh my comment sounded, I quickly added, "To be forced to do the event for free, not…well…you know."

Ruby laughed again. "I knew what you meant, dear. Now the only holdup to rescheduling the event is finding someone willing to cater the thing."

"I don't mean to change the subject," I said, "but I wanted to let you know I'm having a sale on shirtwaist dresses and shorts sets."

"I don't think my legs are see-worthy enough for those shorts sets, but I'll be down to take a look at the dresses in a little while. Thanks for letting me know."

As I was getting ready to call Sarah Conrad, Connie came in.

"Good morning." She gave me a bright smile. "I saw the sign in the hall and wanted to browse."

"I can put Jazzy in her carrier if you'd like to leave the door open."

"That won't be necessary. I should be able to hear if anyone comes in. Thank you, though."

I led her over to the clearance rack and then left her to browse in peace. She soon called out that her daughter, Marielle, would love one of the shorts sets.

Bringing two with her, she held both up. "Which do you think she'd like best?"

One was made of a light blue fabric sprinkled with tiny daisies, and the other was pink with white stripes.

"She'd look adorable in either, but I'm partial to the one with the daisies," I said.

"Me too." She returned the pink one to the rack. "I'll tell some of the other moms about these. When their daughters see Marielle in this, they're going to want some too."

"Thank you. Word of mouth is the best form of advertising."

"I'm sorry the masquerade ball was such a disaster. You worked so hard on those gowns."

Why was everyone acting as if it was *my* event? I still got paid for the gowns I'd made.

"Apparently, the historical society is trying to get the event rescheduled." I smiled. "You don't happen to know a good caterer, do you?"

"I do, and after the way they treated her, she'll never be willing to work with the Brea Ridge Historical Society ever again."

"Oh. I'm sorry."

Connie waved away my apology. "You couldn't know. My friend was supposed to cater the masquerade ball, and then Preston Diggs made those horrible allegations against her. Rather than contacting Betsy and hearing her side of the story, the historical society simply fired her."

"That's terrible," I said.

"Not only that, they put the allegations in their newsletter and sent it out to all their members, tarnishing Betsy's reputation. It's infuriating! What if someone put in a group letter that they'd heard you bought your fabric from a child-labor sweatshop or that you used inferior material?"

"I'd be devastated."

"Betsy was too." She shook her head. "I'm sorry, Amanda. I didn't mean to come across so vociferously. I get protective of my friends."

"I know." I smiled. "It's one of the things everyone loves about you."

Max arrived after Connie left.

"Did you hear any of that?" I asked quietly.

"Yeah, I was here for most of it. Are you thinking what I'm thinking?"

"I'm usually afraid to even ask what you're thinking," I said.

"I'm thinking we need to talk to this tomato who was squished by the historical society—and by *we*, I mean *you*. Unless you can get her here to Designs on You." She perked up. "You could offer her a free dress—one of those shirtwaists you've got on sale."

"And how would that conversation go? 'Hi, I'm Amanda Tucker. You don't know me, but I heard the BRHS treated you like garbage, and I feel sorry for you. Want a free clearance item?'"

Max spread her arms as she shrugged. "If you made *me* that offer, sister, I'd at least come down and eyeball the goods."

"We don't even know the name of the company. All we've got is *Betsy*."

"Then find out the name of the company, cookie. We need to see if she's the one who bumped off Preston Diggs."

"You sure have a lot of confidence in the power of a free shirtdress," I told her. "Not only will it get her here; if she's guilty, it'll make her confess."

"They're gorgeous. I'd tell you a secret for one of them." She grinned. "Wanna hear a secret?"

"I don't know. Do I?"

She nodded. "I think Monica is on the nut."

I frowned. "What kind of nut?"

"On the nut. You know, broke."

"Really?"

"Yeah. I think that's the main reason she wants Dave to pull up stakes and vamoose with her," she said. "She acts like she doesn't want to live with her son because she needs her own space, but I'm betting he's the one who doesn't want her living with him."

"How do you know all of this?"

"I heard Monica talking on the phone to one of her friends. The friend's name was Janey, and she said *she'd* go with Monica if her children weren't here. And then Janey griped about how they don't come to see her enough until Monica got tired of listening to Janey jawing about her problems when hers were so much more important." Max rolled her eyes. "So Monica told Janey that she'd had to pay rent on the shop while she was in Nebraska with her family even though she wasn't doing any business whatsoever."

"Wait. Doesn't she have an online shop?" I asked.

"Who knows? Who even cares? I'm just eager to see her ankle on out of this place without Dave on her arm."

"Surely she realizes that if she leaves here before her lease is up, she'll have to either pay for the rest of the time under contract or find someone to take over her shop."

"Yeah, yeah." Max nodded. "She whined about that to Janey too—tried to get her to open up the window treatment business she was always talking about."

"Window treatments? That sounds interesting."

"Forget it. Janey wasn't interested—said she can't afford it." She patted her hair. "You get back to whatever you were doing, darling. I'm going back to snooping."

I went back to my desk where my laptop was still opened and searched social media for a caterer near me plus the name *Betsy*. Misty Ridge Catering immediately came up in the search. I visited the page and saw posts Betsy had made about being excited to cater the Brea Ridge Historical Society masquerade ball.

Bingo.

Grabbing a pen, I wrote down the address for Misty Ridge Catering and decided to go there when I got off work.

Chapter Twelve

When Maggie brought Zoe into the shop after school, she came in with her. That was oddity number one. Oddity number two was when she spoke with both me and Max as if that happened every day.

Max and I greeted Zoe and Maggie, and I tried not to show my surprise at Maggie's continued civility. I mean, sure, she was friendly at Grandpa's house, but I didn't really expect her to keep it up based on past experience.

"I'm sorry for the way I've treated you," Maggie said. "Aunt Max, you can't help that you're—"

"Dead," Max supplied, as Maggie struggled for the most delicate way to phrase Max's condition.

"Right. And, Amanda, you can't help the circumstances that got you involved in those other murder investigations. I thought you were a nosy, dangerous influence on my daughter, but I see now that you simply want to help people and make sure justice is done."

"Thank you. I—"

Maggie interrupted, and I realized I should have kept quiet until Maggie had finished the speech she was having such difficulty delivering. Naturally, it would be hard for a woman as headstrong as Maggie to admit she was wrong.

"All this is to say I'd like to join your book club Zoe was telling me about."

"Yeah, I told her we should read Victoria Holt's books and then explore her pseudonyms—Jean Plaidy, Philippa Carr, and even Elbur Ford," Zoe said.

"Of course," Max said.

Before any of us could continue the book club discussion, there was a tap on the door, and then Ruby Mills walked into Designs on You.

"Hi, Ruby," I said. "Thank you for coming by."

"Don't let me interrupt your conversation." She held up her hands defensively. "I'm here to check out those dresses you have on sale."

"You're certainly not interrupting." I gestured toward Maggie. "This is Maggie, Zoe's mom. Maggie, this is Ruby Mills."

"Nice to meet you, Maggie. Your daughter certainly is a treasure. Those hats she made for the RenFaire were spectacular. And then the masks she coordinated with Amanda's custom gowns? Absolutely priceless. There's no stopping that young lady from going anywhere and everywhere she wants to go."

Cheeks reddening, Zoe said, "Thank you, Ms. Mills."

"Yes, thank you," Maggie said.

"Ruby, you might be able to help us with something," I said. "Maggie was working with the caterer and was in the kitchen area when Preston Diggs was killed. She said there were some other people she believed to be from the historical society there who had come to ask Mr. Diggs about the food or something."

Nodding, Ruby asked, "How can I help?"

"I don't know their names, but I feel sure I'd recognize their faces," Maggie said. "Since I found Mr. Diggs, the police are looking at me as a suspect. If one of the people who was there saw me and knows I'm innocent, I believe their testimony would help me to prove I didn't hurt Mr. Diggs."

"Then let's figure out who it was you saw." Ruby took out her phone and pulled up the Brea Ridge Historical Society website. She opened a page from the menu and found a group photo. Moving her fingers on the photograph to enlarge it, she said, "See if it was one of these people. That should be all of us."

Although Max was looking over Ruby's shoulder at the photograph, she was being uncharacteristically quiet and unobtrusive. I was guessing the ghostly fashionista was trying not to spook Maggie.

Maggie stepped closer to Ruby, and together they looked at the photograph on her phone.

Pointing, Maggie said, "I'm sure she was one of them."

"That's Jill Eller," Ruby said. "Was she griping about the food?"

"Yes."

"Figures. She takes forever to order in a restaurant." Ruby shook her head. "If she orders a salad, she wants to know exactly what's in the salad, if the ingredients are organic, the name of the chicken that laid the egg, and the sous chef who boiled that egg and cut it up to put it into the dish. She's a good gal and everything, but sometimes a salad is just a salad, and no one needs to know that the chicken's name is Heloise."

Zoe laughed. "Now I want to meet Heloise!"

Ruby tutted. "You would! Who else did you see, Maggie?"

"This one." She pointed to another person.

"Norman. I imagine he wanted to know if any of the food was prepared with alcohol?" When Maggie nodded, Ruby continued, "He had to go to rehab a few years ago, and now he wants to stay as far away from alcohol as humanly possible. I get it, but we've tried to tell him that when wine is used in preparing food, most of the alcohol gets burned away. Still, he swears there are reports that say that isn't true. Either way, I respect his battle."

"Me too." Maggie slid her finger over to the right of Ruby's screen. "I think this man was there as well. He was wearing his mask at the time, but I recognize this scar on his chin."

"Really?" Ruby squinted at Maggie. "Are you certain?"

"Well, I wouldn't swear to it, but I am fairly sure he's the man I saw. That triangular scar is distinctive."

"Huh." Ruby peered down at the photo.

"Who is he, Ruby?" I asked.

"Harry McCall." She turned to me. "Remember I told you about the girl who'd been done so dirty by the society and that her dad was an attorney?"

"Yes, I remember."

"Harry is Betsy's dad," Ruby said. "I'm very surprised to learn that he was at the ball. I suppose he might've put in an appearance to support the BRHS, but I really thought the whole nasty business with his daughter would make him break off ties to the society."

"Well, thank you for your help," Maggie said. "I'll let you go on and shop now."

As Ruby shopped the sales rack, Zoe and Maggie went into the atelier.

It wasn't until after Ruby had left that Maggie and Zoe rejoined Max and me in the reception area.

"I want to let you know I've already looked up Misty Ridge Catering," I said, "and I'm planning to go by the business office after work to see if I can speak with Betsy, the owner, about the masquerade ball fiasco."

"Now that you know the dame's dad was milling around in the kitchen area at the time of Preston Diggs's death, you can ask her about that too," Max said.

"True." I straightened a stack of business cards near the credit card reader. "I'm also going to call Detective Cranston to see if we can meet. He's on the Abingdon force, but I believe he can still look into the case and see if my theory about Mr. Diggs being poisoned prior to being stabbed holds water."

"I appreciate your going to all that trouble for me," Maggie said.

"That's what friends do," I told her.

"And family," Max added.

"Maybe I can go with you," Maggie said.

"Yeah." I didn't want her to go with me.

With Max, Maggie, and Zoe chatting in the reception area, I wandered through the atelier, into the hallway, and up the stairs to Jason's studio. Opening the door slightly, I peeped inside to make sure he wasn't with a client.

He looked up from his computer screen. "Hey, beautiful. This is a nice surprise."

We tried not to disturb each other too often during the day. It wasn't terribly hard since we both had businesses to run. The difficulty was usually in making time for each other.

I went on into his studio, closed the door, and gave him a proper kiss hello. He took my hand and led me over to one of his prop sofas—the leather one.

"What's on your mind?" he asked.

"You."

He raised a brow.

"You *are* on my mind," I insisted.

"Okay, but there's something else going on too. I can see it written all over your face."

Slumping back against the cushions, I said, "I intended to do a little sleuthing after work today."

"As you are wont to do."

"And I wanted to do it alone, but now Maggie wants to go with me."

"Makes sense," he said. "I take it you're sleuthing on her behalf?"

"Yes. And I don't know why I'm bothered by this. She's never liked me before, and now she's extending not only an olive branch but the whole darn tree, and I have mixed feelings. Why is that?"

"I can think of a few reasons." He put his arm along the back of the couch. "You might be afraid her kindness won't last, and that after this crisis is resolved, she'll go back to not liking you."

"Could be."

"It could be that you don't feel comfortable around her yet," he said. "I don't mean you're suspicious of her or anything, but you don't actually know her."

"That's true too."

"And, last but not least, you might be afraid that a friendship with Maggie could alter your relationship with Zoe."

I frowned. "In what way?"

"Well, you've always been something of a cool big sister to Zoe—a mentor and confidante. If you become friends with her mother, she might become reluctant to confide in you. She may begin to see you as more of her mother's friend than her friend."

"That's a good point." I caressed his face. "You should moonlight as a therapist."

Chuckling, he said, "Sometimes I feel like I do."

"I feel you're right in that I don't want to disrupt the way things are now." I meant that not only with regard to

Zoe but also to Max. Currently, I felt I held a special place with both of them, and I didn't want to be replaced—especially not now when Grandpa Dave was considering leaving. "How messed up is that?"

Jason kissed my head. "It isn't messed up at all, sweetheart. It's human. If you *knew* you could have a friend in Maggie and have the relationship with Zoe either remain the same or be strengthened, then you'd be fine. You'd welcome Maggie's friendship."

"So, what do I do?

"You sit down and talk with her. Remind her that she's important to you and always will be."

"You're a wonderful boyfriend, you know that?"

"Mmm-hmmm."

Resting my head against his chest, I asked, "May I stay for five more minutes? Then I promise I'll get back to work."

"Stay for as long as you'd like."

Chapter Thirteen

I went into the kitchen to make a cup of kava tea to soothe my nerves. There was no one else in the room until Max came in and perched atop the refrigerator.

"Must you?" I asked softly. "That brings to mind Biscuit leaping onto my head on Saturday."

"Sorry." She slid onto the floor. "I wanted to make sure you're all right."

"I'm fine. Why?"

"I know you aren't," she said.

The microwave dinged. I removed my cup of water and placed the tea bag into it to steep.

"Were you eavesdropping on Jason and me?"

Her face hardened. "I'd never do that."

"Then how did you know something was wrong?"

She pressed her lips together into a hard line. "Listen, kiddo, I've been dead far longer than you've been alive, and I'm a great observer of people. Especially those I care about. That's how I knew something was bothering you. But I'll butt out."

I sighed and ran a hand over my face. "Max—"

She was gone. I guessed she'd returned to the shop. I didn't want to talk with her in front of Zoe and Maggie, but I would apologize at least; and I'd tell her I'm upset about Grandpa. At least, that wouldn't be a complete untruth.

Ford came into the kitchen then for a cup of coffee. "Hey, there. Everything okay?"

"Just a little stressed." I gave him a tight smile. "I hope the kava will help."

"Yeah, it's good stuff." He nodded toward his ceramic book-lover's mug. "You're trying to wind down, and I'm trying to wake up."

Remembering the promise I made to Joey Conrad, I asked, "Do you have anything you'd recommend for Joey Conrad?" No one at Shops on Main was unfamiliar with Joey and the ferrets. "I promised him a new book for helping me catch Biscuit the other day."

"You do know that's his pet and that it's kind of his job to look after it, don't you?"

"I do." I grinned. "But in this instance, it jumped from the top of the fridge onto my head, so I was so relieved to have it captured that I promised Joey a book without even thinking about it." That wasn't *exactly* how that situation went, but it was close enough.

"Sure. I'll look through my inventory and see what I've got that isn't *too* antiquated," he said.

"Thanks." I dropped my tea bag into the trash can and went into Designs on You.

I'd hoped Max would be in the atelier so I could speak with her privately before we joined Zoe and Maggie in the reception area, but she wasn't there. Unfortunately, she wasn't in the reception area either.

"Where's Max?" Zoe asked, as I walked over to my desk.

"I don't know. I hope she's upstairs, but…." I sat my tea on a coaster and then sat on the chair. "She's upset with me."

"What happened?"

"She said something that made me think she might've been eavesdropping on my conversation with Jason."

"Max wouldn't do that," Zoe said.

"I know. I just—" I sighed. "I've been so on edge lately with this entire situation with Grandpa."

"What situation?" Maggie asked. "Is Dave all right?"

While I explained to Maggie that Monica was trying to convince Grandpa to move to Nebraska with her, Zoe went upstairs to look for Max.

"If it's any consolation, I don't believe he'll go," Maggie said when I'd finished. "He has too great a life here. I could see him leaving if he was lonely and had nothing and no one other than this Monica, but he does. He lives a busy, active, exciting life."

"Maybe that's why she wants him to go with her."

"Maybe it is. Does he often have Monica over for Sunday lunch?"

"No," I said. "Often Max joins us, and there's no way we could talk with her if Monica was there. Sunday lunch is sometimes the only opportunity Grandpa has to chat with Max."

"So Max means more to Dave than Monica does."

"I wouldn't say that." I frowned. "But I guess I wouldn't *not* say that either. Huh. I hadn't thought about that."

Maggie smiled slightly. "I understand. You're letting your emotions cloud your logic. I've done that a few times myself."

Zoe came back downstairs and declared that she couldn't find Max anywhere. "I even went into Monica's shop. Give the woman her due, she does have some pretty cool stuff in her shop. There was nothing I'd really want to take home, even though she was giving me the hard sell."

"Eager to sell everything so she can leave, I guess," I said.

"I suppose." Zoe flopped onto one of the wingback chairs. "I'm sorry you argued with Max."

"Me too." I wrote I'M SORRY in the notes app on her tablet and left it open so it would be the first thing she'd see when she turned it on. It was almost closing time, and I didn't want to forget to apologize before I left.

Ford knocked on the atelier door and then came on through to the reception area. He had a few books in his hands.

"Hey, there." He placed the books on the corner of my desk. "This is what I could find that I thought might appeal to Joey." He glanced around at Zoe and then his eyes fell on Maggie. "Am I interrupting anything?"

"No. Ford, haven't you met Maggie, Zoe's mom?" I asked.

"I haven't had the pleasure." He shook Maggie's hand. "It's nice to meet you."

"Likewise. I've heard Zoe say a lot of good things about you."

"Thanks." He continued staring at Maggie until I interrupted him.

"So, what've you got?" I asked.

"Oh, yeah." He turned back to the small stack of books. "I have the 1911 classic edition of *Peter Pan*, by J. M. Barrie; *The Wind in the Willows* by Kenneth Grahame; and book one in *The Secret Seven* series by Enid Blyton."

"*The Secret Seven*," I said. "I read every *Secret Seven* book I could get my hands on when I was a kid."

"All right. Here you go." He handed me the book off the stack, and I sat there smiling at it like an idiot. "I have another copy upstairs, if you'd like this one for yourself."

"No, that's okay. Although I might reread it before I pass it on to Joey." I got my purse and paid Ford for the book. "Thanks for bringing these down."

"You're welcome." He picked up the remaining titles, tucked them under his arm, and turned to Maggie. "It was a pleasure to meet you. I hope I'll see you around again sometime."

"I hope so too," she said.

Zoe and I exchanged raised-eyebrow looks, but we both kept our mouths shut.

Misty Ridge Catering was located in a brick building that was part of a strip mall that was seeking to revitalize an underused part of town. The dark-red brick building wasn't what I was anticipating, but then I wasn't sure exactly what the exterior of a catering business was supposed to look like.

The interior was much more appropriate to the business. In the reception area, there was a long white sofa, two club chairs, an elegant oval glass-topped coffee table, and a matching side table beside one of the chairs. The side table contained easels holding business cards and glossy flyers. There was dark blue carpet on the floor and a Persian runner rug in the hallway that led to rooms to the left of the reception area.

A bell had sounded when Zoe, Maggie, and I had walked into the building, but there was also a Victorian-style call bell on the cherry desk that faced the door.

"Should we ring that?" Zoe asked.

"No," Maggie hissed.

I tended to agree but said nothing. I simply hoped Betsy or whomever would come to speak with us soon. If not, I'd prefer to leave and come back another time. Actually, I hoped that's what would happen. I'd have liked to have spoken with Betsy alone. How likely was she to open up to the woman suspected of killing Preston Diggs, that woman's daughter, and another complete stranger? Had I come alone to say I was throwing a party for my grandfather, then I might have been able to get her to open up.

"Welcome to Misty Ridge Catering." The woman who stepped into the reception area appeared to have been in her early- to mid-forties. She gave us a bright smile. "How may I help you today?"

"Hi, I'm Amanda Tucker, and I'm considering throwing a party for my grandfather."

"Oh, that's great." She gestured toward the seating area. "Please go on over and make yourselves comfortable. I'm Betsy Jameson, by the way. Let me grab my tablet."

Maggie and Zoe sat on the sofa, and I sat on one of the chairs, leaving the one next to the table for Betsy.

When Betsy sat down, she immediately opened the tablet. I supposed she had some sort of app that allowed her to quickly prepare an estimate for potential clients. I used something similar myself.

"Is your grandfather celebrating a special birthday?" Betsy asked.

"No." I folded my hands in my lap. "He's considering getting married."

"How wonderful!" Her smile slowly faded when no one echoed her sentiments. "You aren't happy about it?"

"I'm not sure," I said. "I might be if the marriage didn't include him moving halfway across the country."

"Oooh." Betsy pursed her lips. "That's hard. Still, it's terribly thoughtful of you to want to have a party for him."

"If he goes, I'll definitely throw him a party," I said. "But if he stays, I'll be tempted to throw him an even bigger one."

Betsy forced out a laugh. "Let's get started, shall we? How many guests do you expect?"

"Before we get into all that," Maggie began.

My stomach felt as if it was plummeting to the floor.

"—what's the story behind that Brea Ridge Historical Society masquerade ball fiasco?"

Betsy looked as if she'd been made to feel as queasy as I had by Maggie's question. "Whatever you've heard, it was untrue. In fact, had we not settled out of court, I was going to sue for those food poisoning rumors."

"Yes, we heard your father was going to sue?" Maggie asked.

"He was. Harry McCall is one of the best attorneys around, and he was going to see to it that both Renata Crenshaw and Preston Diggs paid dearly for spreading unfounded gossip about me and Misty Ridge Catering."

"Then why was your father at the ball?" Maggie simply would not let up.

I sat there and wished she would hush. The subtle approach was entirely foreign to Maggie Flannagan. Why hadn't I insisted on coming here alone?

"He wasn't," Betsy said stiffly.

"He was," Maggie said. "I saw him there."

"I don't know who you are or what your true intention was in coming here, but you need to leave. Now. If you're still here when I return, I'm calling the police." Betsy stood and stormed out of the reception area and down the hall.

Chapter Fourteen

I'd just finished having ice cream for dinner when Jason called to ask how the meeting with the caterer went.

"Guess what I had for dinner, and you'll know," I said.

"Ice cream?"

"You got it."

"That bad, huh?"

I told him how Maggie had immediately started grilling Betsy as if she were Kyra Sedgwick in a particularly tense episode of *The Closer*. "Oh, Jason, it was awful. 'What was that whole masquerade ball fiasco about? Why was your father at the ball?' Betsy didn't even know he'd been there. Naturally, she threw us out."

"Maybe you can go back and talk to her on your own."

Sighing, I said, "I doubt it. I'm afraid now she'd call the police on sight, even if I was waving a stack of cash in her face and saying I wanted to use it for a deposit. I mean, I started out so well. I was going to get an estimate for a reception in case Grandpa *does* decide to marry Monica and move to Nebraska with her. I even told Betsy I might throw him an even bigger party if he doesn't marry Monica."

"Sounds like you had an excellent plan."

"I did! And then Maggie stepped right in and blew it." I groaned. "It was awful." I thought a moment. "I suppose I *could* call her and apologize for Maggie's behavior, say I had no idea what she was going to say—which, obviously if I *had*, I'd have told her flat out that she couldn't go with me—and ask if she'd see me privately for that quote for Grandpa's party."

"I think that would work well. There are a lot of times I have a couple or a group, and one person acts like a complete jerk. I never hold it against the innocent parties, and sometimes I learn that the person who was obnoxious behaved that way because of a simple misunderstanding."

"That's true. I could tell Betsy that it was Maggie who found Preston Diggs's body and that she was freaked out about his death."

"Right," he said. "Or maybe don't bring up the ball again at all. Merely apologize for Maggie's behavior, assure Betsy that Maggie won't be a part of the planning process, and ask if you can meet with her again. Because even though I sometimes understand why a person acted in a way I didn't appreciate, that doesn't mean I want to work with them again."

"Talking with you always makes me feel better. I wish I'd talked with you before I ate an entire pint of moose tracks ice cream. That's making me feel rather blah right now."

He chuckled. "You'll be all right. And my calendar is free tomorrow evening. If you don't have something planned already, I'd love to take you for a more substantial dinner."

"You're on. Oh, by the way, Ford brought some books by Designs on You today and met Maggie for the first time. They seemed attracted to each other. I wondered if I should—"

"No," he interrupted. "You definitely should not. The matchmaker always gets burned."

"C'mon. Not *always*."

"Most of the time. Do you want to run the risk of losing the friendship of Ford, Maggie, or both?"

"No, you know I don't," I said.

"Then stay out of it. If they're interested, they'll find a way to get together without your involvement."

"Once again, you're filled with excellent advice."

"Advice is so much easier to give than to take," he said. "But staying out of other people's relationships is one I wish I had taken more than once. Let's just say I've learned my lesson."

After talking with Jason, I started to call Grandpa Dave, but I decided to wait until tomorrow morning. I didn't want to appear too clingy. I truly wanted him to follow his heart, and I desperately hoped his heart would convince him to stay here in Abingdon. But I didn't want to guilt him into staying because he thought I couldn't survive here on my own. Because, of course, I could—I just didn't want to.

Then I checked to see if Max was online. She wasn't. I decided that conversation could also wait until tomorrow.

Despite the fact that today had been the least busy day I'd spent at work in months, I felt exhausted. My fatigue was probably a residual effect of my frantic days and evenings getting everything ready for the masquerade ball. I went to bed early with my copy of *Bride of Pendorric*.

I went in to Designs on You early Tuesday morning. I wanted to get there before everyone else so I could speak with Max. Unfortunately, she wasn't there. Had I made her so angry that she'd decided not to talk with me again?

"Max? Max? Are you here?"

Nothing.

After getting Jazzy settled for the day, I got out my sketchbook, sat by the window, and began working on a 1930s-style suit with a pleated skirt and embroidered accents on the left lapel of the cuffed-sleeve jacket.

I was startled by a knock on the window. There was a man standing on the porch.

"I can't get inside!" he called.

"Shops on Main isn't open yet. We—"

"I'm looking for Amanda Tucker!"

"I'm Amanda. What can I do for you?"

"I'm Harry McCall, and I'm here about my daughter, Betsy."

"I'll come outside." The other vendors would be coming in soon, but I didn't want to be alone with a stranger inside Shops on Main for any length of time. I'd prefer to be on the porch where someone on the busy road would surely see if he assaulted me. After all, we didn't know that he wasn't the person who stabbed Preston Diggs.

Setting my sketchbook aside, I went out the reception area door and closed it back so Jazzy couldn't follow. Then I unlocked the front door and stepped onto the porch. "How may I help you, Mr. McCall?"

"What did you mean telling my daughter that I went to that wretched masquerade ball?"

"Actually, it was my friend, Maggie, who mentioned that. I believe she thought Betsy knew." It might have been cowardly to throw Maggie under the bus, but this man was here, angry, and possibly guilty of the murder of Preston Diggs. Besides that, I *wasn't* the one who told Betsy he was at the ball.

"Of course, she didn't know! I'd recently threatened to sue the historical society on her behalf for their shoddy treatment of her!"

I tucked a strand of windblown hair behind my ear. "I'm sorry. For all of it. I hate that Betsy was maligned by the historical society, and I'm sorry Maggie mentioned to her that you were there." I took a moment to gather up my nerve. "Why *did* you go?"

"Not that it's any of your business, but I've been a vital part of the Brea Ridge Historical Society for most of my life, as was my father before me," he said. "Rather than throw away a lifetime of service to the society due to Preston Diggs's manipulation and Renata Crenshaw's stupidity, the best thing I can do is fight for the society and make sure Renata is voted out of office."

"And what about Mr. Diggs?" I asked.

His face reddened. "I was determined to see that jackass fall on his face. Hot Diggity, indeed. The restaurant bills itself as being a little bit of everything—

well, it's a whole lot of nothing, if you want my opinion. Had someone not done the man in, I'd have made certain he paid for what he did to my daughter."

Needing to know why he was in the kitchen area, I took a huge leap. "Is that what you were talking with him about that evening?"

The red in his face deepened to a purplish hue. He took a step toward me, and I instinctively stepped back. I was afraid he might strike me.

Max appeared between us. She couldn't keep him from hitting me, but she had her arms outstretched and was doing everything she could to make him keep his distance. The door alarm went off.

"About time," she muttered. "I tried to make that blasted thing go off before I came out here."

"I don't know what you're getting at, young lady!" Mr. McCall yelled above the din of the alarm. "But you'd better not be insinuating I had anything to do with Diggs's death! And if there's any reason I can come up with to sue you, you can bet I'll do it! I'll ruin you, Amanda Tucker!"

Thankfully, once he'd said his piece—or, rather, *shouted* it—he left.

I turned, went back inside, and shut off the alarm. "Thanks, Max." My voice was barely above a whisper.

"It'll be okay. He's just an old blowhard."

"A blowhard who could cost me everything I've got." I sank onto the chair I'd vacated when Mr. McCall knocked on the window. "He's a vindictive, spiteful old man who believes I hurt his daughter's feelings. He said he'd ruin me, and I don't doubt he'll try."

"But, darling, you've done nothing wrong. You went into his daughter's catering business to get an estimate—a legitimate reason for going there. He's the one who came here and acted like a hood."

"I don't have to have done something wrong for him to sue me." I buried my face in my hands. "Why didn't I stay out of it?"

"Because it was Maggie…and Zoe." She paused. "And it just ain't in you to stay out of stuff."

Raising my head, I said, "I'm sorry about yesterday."

"I know. I didn't hold it against you." She gave me a half shrug. "I *do* eavesdrop. On just about everybody in this building. But not you." She grinned. "I don't have to. You always tell me everything eventually."

I laughed. "I do, don't I?"

There was a knock on the door, and I stiffened.

"It's Dave," Max said. "I called him as soon as you went outside to talk to the palooka that knocked on the window."

I blew out a breath of relief as I stood, unlocked the door, opened it, and hugged Grandpa Dave.

"Are you all right, Pup? Max said there was an angry-looking goon outside and that you went to confront him on your own."

"It was Hank McCall," I said. "He threatened to ruin me."

"Hank McCall is an A-number-one jerk. He'll regret harassing my granddaughter." He looked down at me. "Is everything okay?"

"I'm fine. Shook up a little, but that's it."

"Good. I'm going to have a word with Hank."

"Grandpa, don't. It's not worth it."

He kissed my forehead. "I'll be back soon." He stalked back out the front door.

It was close enough to time for Shops on Main to open that I didn't lock it back again. Max and I returned to Designs on You.

"What do you think he's gonna do?" I asked softly.

"I don't know, but I sure wish I could go with him and watch." She placed the back of her hand on her forehead and pretended to swoon. "That man makes me wish I wasn't dead."

"About Maggie," I began, wanting to make sure I'd cleared the air with Max before anyone else arrived at Shops on Main, "I'm sorry for throwing her under the bus with Harry McCall."

She waved away my concerns with a flick of her wrist. "Zoe told me everything last night. She was mortified that her mother behaved the way she did at Misty Ridge Catering. Zoe felt like Betsy probably didn't deserve that, and I agree. She'd already been put through enough, and

I'm guessing you were trying to handle her with kid gloves."

"I was. I was mainly hoping she could tell me more about Preston Diggs, about other people whose reputations he might have damaged, about his enemies." I blew out a breath. "But I also understand Maggie getting impatient and wanting an immediate answer to the question of who really killed Mr. Diggs. Until his murderer is revealed, Maggie is still at the heart of the investigation."

"I know. She didn't get on our chat. I believe she was talking with Dwight." She looked down at the floor. "I didn't mention this to Zoe—and don't you—but I'm pretty sure she was talking with Dwight about what to do if she gets framed for this crime."

My jaw dropped. "She told you that?"

"No, but something Dwight said later gave me that impression."

"It'll be okay," I said. "It has to be."

I sincerely hoped I wasn't lying to my best friend.

Chapter Fifteen

Other vendors began arriving at Shops on Main. I put aside my sketchbook and went over to speak with Connie.

"Good morning," I said.

She greeted me with a warm smile. "Hi. How are you?"

"Well, I'm fine now, but I was rather shaken up this morning." I told her about what happened with Harry McCall.

"That's terrible!" She opened a package that had been delivered late yesterday afternoon, not appearing too concerned about the incident.

"How well do you know the McCall family?"

"Well, I know Betsy—she and I went to school together—but I don't really know the rest of her family.

Harry has the reputation of being something of a bulldog." She began taking jar candles out of the box. "I'll give Betsy a call and explain that Maggie was upset, that she'd found the body, and that—" She spread her hands. "That Maggie can be abrupt."

"Thanks, Connie. I'd appreciate that. I mainly want Betsy to know that I didn't mean her any harm and that I was interested in a party for Grandpa."

"You don't really think he'll leave, do you?"

I shrugged. "I hope not."

Giving me a sympathetic smile, she said, "Me, too."

Max was perched on the desk with Jazzy lying beside her. They were both apparently waiting for my full report on the visit with Connie.

"She's going to call Betsy and try to explain," I said, resuming my seat in the chair by the window and picking up the sketchbook.

"Fat lot of good that'll do."

Grandpa Dave returned. "I don't think Mr. McCall will be giving you any more trouble, Pup."

Max hopped off the desk, bounced on the balls of her feet, and put up her fists. "Did you give that goon the old one-two?" She threw a couple of punches to demonstrate.

Laughing, he sat down in the chair to my right. "I didn't have to. I threatened—make that *promised*—to report him to the Virginia State Bar for harassing Amanda at her place of employment and to finance her suit against him for stalking her should he ever come around her or slander her."

I let out a breath I hadn't realized I'd been holding since Grandpa had come into the reception area. "So, everything is going to be all right now?"

"Yep."

"I still wish you'd given him the old one-two," Max said, "but I understand why you didn't."

There was a tap on the door before Connie came inside. "Good morning, Dave. How are you?"

"Finer than a frog's hair split three ways." He grinned. "How are you, Connie?"

"I'm well, thanks. Amanda, I spoke with Betsy. She understands that you weren't at fault, and she was appalled that her father came here to confront you this morning. She said she'd give him a good talking to."

Monica came into Designs on You through the atelier entrance and strode on into the reception area. "Dave, I saw your truck here. What's the occasion?"

"I'd better get back," Connie said. "I hope you all have a lovely day."

"You, too." I waited until Connie had closed the door before saying, "Grandpa is here being my knight in shining armor and saving the day." I gave him a broad smile.

Arching her brows, Monica said, "You know, some women prefer to stop being damsels and save themselves."

"And *some* women prefer to give know-it-alls the old one-two!" Max punched at Monica. Even though the punches couldn't land, I think it made Max feel better.

"Shew," Monica said. "Why do you keep it so cold in here?"

I merely shrugged.

Grandpa had his head down and was shaking with suppressed laughter.

"Dave, are we still on for lunch?" she asked.

He nodded but didn't raise his eyes to hers.

"See you then," she said. "Amanda, think about what I said." She left, not knowing that Max was still throwing hands in her direction.

When Monica got out of the atelier and into the hall, we all burst into laughter.

"Maxine Englebright," Grandpa said, wiping his eyes as he stood. "That was the funniest thing I've seen in ages."

"Glad I could entertain you, Silver Fox." She winked.

He gave me a peck on the cheek. "I'll see you later. Want me to bring you some lunch?"

"I don't know. Don't *some women* have to fend for themselves?" I asked.

"Some women aren't my granddaughter."

Max applauded, and he took a bow before leaving.

Renata Crenshaw came into the shop about an hour after Grandpa Dave had left. I didn't know where Max was at the moment, but I wouldn't have been surprised to learn that she was upstairs snooping on Monica—or still trying to give her the old one-two.

"Good morning, Amanda."

"Good morning, Ms. Crenshaw. How are you today?"

"I must admit I'm a bit annoyed. Ruby told me you were having a sale; and even though I'm put out that you didn't invite me yourself, I'm here to look at those shirtdresses."

"I started to call you," I said, "but you've had so much on your mind that I hated to bother you. I'm glad you stopped in though."

"And I appreciate your consideration." She patted her hair. "It has been difficult. All of it."

She sank onto one of the navy chairs by the window, and I sat on the chair beside her.

"I'm sure it has been," I said. "Is there anything I can do to help?"

"Well…you might knock an extra ten percent off one of those shirtdresses if I find one I like."

It took some supreme effort on my part not to roll my eyes, and I was relieved Max wasn't there to add her special brand of commentary.

"Of course, I will," I said.

"Thank you." She sniffed.

"What can you tell me about Harry McCall?" I asked.

"He's a jerk. Why?"

I told her about going to see Mr. McCall's daughter at her catering business, inadvertently upsetting her, and then Mr. McCall coming here this morning.

"So, wait." She leaned forward in her chair. "He was at the ball?"

"Yes. Maggie saw him there prior to her finding Mr. Diggs lying on the floor with the knife in his chest."

"Would she be willing to testify that Harry stabbed Preston?"

"No," I said. "She didn't see what happened to Mr. Diggs."

"But she *thinks* Harry stabbed him?"

"I never said that." Why was this woman so intent on twisting my words? Was she that eager to have Harry arrested for Preston Diggs's murder? If so, why? Did she know who did kill the man? Or did she just hate Harry that much? "Have the police confirmed that stabbing was the cause of death?"

"Not to me, but how else would he have died? It was obvious he was stabbed. The killer left the knife sticking out of his chest."

"What if he was poisoned and then stabbed to cover up the actual cause of death?" I asked.

"That's ridiculous. Unless he poisoned himself eating some of that trash he calls food."

I frowned. "If you feel that his food is trash, then why did you agree to allow him to cater the ball?"

"I didn't have much choice, did I? Who else was I going to get at the last minute? There aren't *that* many caterers in this area." She pursed her lips. "I was a fool to believe what he told me about Misty Ridge."

"He said there was an incident of food poisoning?" I spoke softly, wanting her to feel like I was inquiring as a caring acquaintance not interrogating her like a detective.

"Yes—at a wedding he attended a couple of months ago. I knew I was about to incur Harry McCall's wrath by firing his daughter, but I couldn't risk people backing out of the ball because they were afraid to eat the food."

"Of course not," I said. "It sounds as if you were caught between a rock and a hard place—or, rather, between two men you couldn't stand."

"That's true." Her lips curved into a half smile. "How perfect it would be if Harry did kill Preston." She snapped out of her reverie. "Oh, well, I'd better have a look at those shirtdresses."

I stood. “Right this way.”

As soon as Renata Crenshaw left, I called Detective Cranston. He answered on the first ring and agreed to meet me for lunch. I had so many questions I needed answered.

Chapter Sixteen

"Dave's here!" Max called, when she spotted Grandpa pulling into the parking lot.

I hurried to catch him before he went upstairs and motioned him into the reception area.

"Is everything all right?" he asked.

"Everything is fine. I just wanted you to know that I'm buying Detective Cranston lunch, so you don't have to bring me anything back."

"Okay." He drew out the word, obviously wanting an explanation as to why I was buying lunch for a detective who wasn't on the team investigating Preston Diggs's murder.

"He got a promotion after the first case I was involved in, so I figure he owes me. I want to see if my theory that Mr. Diggs was poisoned before he was stabbed holds any water."

"I'm staying here and looking after the cat," Max announced, as if she could do otherwise.

"That's good of you," Grandpa said.

She shrugged. "I'm angelic."

"Anything else you think I should quiz him about?" I asked.

Although I was asking Grandpa, Max answered my question. "Sure. Get the skinny on that palooka Harry McCall. Let him know the creep was yelling at you on the front porch this morning."

"Good thinking," Grandpa said. "I do believe I put him off, but it's always good to have more information. Also, Pup, see if he can find out what the witnesses who were milling around near Preston Diggs at the time of his attack are saying. I find it hard to imagine that no one saw anything."

"I agree." I kissed his cheek. "I'm off. I hope you enjoy your lunch."

He didn't respond. Instead, he walked with me to the stairs and issued a curt "be careful" before walking on up to Monica's collectibles shop.

When I left the building for lunch, I usually asked the other vendors if I could bring them something back.

Today, I didn't do that. Jason was already out taking photographs for a freelance magazine article assignment, and I didn't want anyone else to know where I was going.

Detective Reese Cranston was seated facing the door at a table in the corner of the Down South Café. He was in his mid-to-late forties, sandy haired, blue eyed, and possessed of a perpetual expression of seriousness.

A handsome guy with his hair in a ponytail greeted me when I entered the café. "Sit wherever you'd like. I'll be with you in a moment."

"Thank you," I said. "I see my friend."

I crossed the crowded room to the detective's table. We'd decided to meet in Winter Garden rather than Abingdon so there was less chance of bumping into someone we'd both know.

He was nursing a soda, and there was a menu in front of him. "What's good here?"

"Everything."

Nodding, he glanced down at the menu. "Let's order and then get our business talk out of the way. I have to tell you up front that I can't give away any sensitive information from either our department or the Brea Ridge police department."

"I understand. I don't necessarily want you to tell me what you find out. I only want to know there is someone looking into all the possibilities."

"I do believe you might have missed your calling, Ms. Tucker."

I didn't know about that, but I didn't comment. Instead, I smiled at the waiter, who was walking in our direction.

"Hi, I'm Scott. What would you like to drink?"

"I'll have an iced tea, please, and I'm ready to order."

"Go right ahead then." He raised his pad and pen.

"I'd like a burger and fries."

He grinned. "Well, that's easy enough. Sir, have you made up your mind?"

"I'll have the same," Detective Cranston said.

As soon as Scott walked away, I leaned forward and lowered my voice so that it would become lost in the sea of buzzing conversation and clinking silverware that surrounded us.

"I'd like you to check the possibility that Preston Diggs was poisoned before he was stabbed at the masquerade ball."

Cranston frowned. "I haven't heard any scuttlebutt about that. Why would you think he was poisoned?"

"It all happened so quickly. Wouldn't it take a trained assassin to stab someone once and have that person die immediately?"

"Maybe." He spread his hands. "Maybe the killer got lucky. That makes more sense than to think someone poisoned the guy and followed him around until they got tired of waiting for him to die and then stabbed him."

"I guess." I saw Scott bringing my drink, so I shut up and smiled. "Thank you."

"You're welcome," Scott said, placing my glass on the table. "Your food should be ready soon. If you need anything in the meantime, give me a yell."

I resumed speaking quietly after Scott had left the table. "There are just so many factors in play here. Diggs had accused the caterer hired by the historical society of food poisoning at a wedding he attended. The historical society reported the alleged incident in their newsletter, and one of their members—Harry McCall, who is also the caterer's father—threatened to sue for libel."

"I've heard of McCall. He's got a reputation as an obnoxious bully."

"That's been my experience, but I can tell you about that later. I don't want to get sidetracked," I said. "Well, Maggie Flannagan, who is the Brea Ridge PD's prime suspect because she'd argued with the victim and then found his body, saw Harry McCall in the area at the time Mr. Diggs was stabbed."

"Did she see him with a knife or anything?"

"No. That's what is so confounding about this entire case. Nobody appeared to have seen anything. I'd like for you to look into it, to the extent that you can, and try to—" I broke off.

"Try to clear your friend?" he asked.

"She's innocent. I know she is."

"I have some friends in the Brea Ridge PD. I'll see what I can find out."

"Thanks," I said. "I appreciate your help."

Later that afternoon, I was going through my files for a pattern—or two—that would work for the 1930s-style suit I'd designed. I planned to make one for the mannequin and see how popular it was before making more. Sales were fun, but full price was better for my bottom line.

I heard the reception room door open. "Be right with you!"

"Take your time."

It was an unfamiliar male voice.

Leaving the drawer to the file cabinet open, I stepped out of the atelier. The man had his back to me and was looking out the window.

"May I help you?"

He turned, and I saw it was Tony Diggs. "Hi, Amanda."

"Hey, there." I walked on into the reception area. "How are you holding up?"

"Not good." He sat on the chair in front of my desk. "Do you have a minute?"

"Sure." I was glad he'd sat in front of the desk because that allowed me to sit behind it, making the seating arrangement more formal than it would have been had we sat in the chairs by the window. "I'm terribly sorry about your dad."

"Yeah, me, too." He sighed. "I'm still trying to wrap my head around the whole thing, you know?"

"I can only imagine." *Why had he come here?*

He looked around. "Are you by yourself today?"

"For now." *Was he talking about Zoe? Or clients?* "Mondays and Tuesdays are typically slow. Traffic starts picking up about the middle of the week when people start considering their weekend plans or…or whatever."

"Yeah, sure, but I thought you had that kid who was your assistant or something?"

"Zoe, yeah. She'll be here later."

"It was her mom who found my dad, wasn't it?" he asked.

"Yes. Maggie." I swallowed. "Maggie Flannagan."

Tony leaned forward, placed his elbows on his knees, and looked down at the floor. "I had to make funeral arrangements today."

"I'm sorry. I know how difficult that must have been."

"Mom's gone, you know. It's just me. Only child." His voice broke slightly. "It's all on me."

"That's rough." I was running out of condolences. I mean, I didn't even know this guy. I had no idea what to say that might help or make him feel better.

He raised his head, his eyes brimming with unshed tears. "Will you have dinner with me tonight?"

"Jason and I have reservations already, but I'll be happy to see if we can add a third—or a fourth, if you're bringing a date."

"Don't bother. I was hoping it would only be the two of us and that we could catch up on old times."

"Maybe some other time," I said.

"Yeah." He stood. "I'd better be going. I need to look at the restaurant's books and figure out if I want to keep the place open or not."

"Well, good luck."

He stalked out of the reception area without saying goodbye.

"Wanted to catch up on old times, my Great Aunt Fanny."

I started when I heard Max's voice beside me. I looked up at her. "Do you even *have* a Great Aunt Fanny?"

"Of course, I do!" She turned her back to me and looked over her shoulder. "Now *aunt* that a *great fanny*?"

I joined in her laughter. "That's a good one. I'll have to remember it."

"Sorry, I didn't get here sooner."

"Why? Would you have given Tony the old one-two?"

She grinned. "I might've. I spent some time with Ford to get to know him a little better."

I passed along Jason's warning about matchmakers.

"I'm not going to try to push them together, but I want to find out more about him in case the two of them find each other on their own," she said. "Dave didn't seem very lovey-dovey with Monica when he collected her for lunch. I saw them from the window. Monica tried to take his hand, and he wouldn't let her."

"Huh. Wonder why?"

"Probably because the old trout was rude to you this morning." Max put her hands on her hips. "She might think Dave loves her, but he *adores* his granddaughter. Her big cakehole might have blown her chances with him all to smithereens."

Before I could comment on the old trout's cakehole, my phone rang. "Thank you for calling Designs on You. This is Amanda. How may I help you?"

"Amanda, this is Betsy Jameson from Misty Ridge Catering. I hate that we got off on the wrong foot, and I'd like the chance to meet with you and give you an estimate for your grandfather's party. Are you free this evening?"

"I have plans this evening, but I could leave work a few minutes early and come to Misty Ridge if that would work for you."

"That would be excellent. Thank you for giving me another chance," she said.

"Likewise. See you around four-thirty." After ending the call, I looked at Max. "I suppose you figured out that was Betsy, the caterer."

She nodded. "I could hear her side of the conversation too. I wonder if she's truly making amends or if she's up to something?"

"I'll soon find out."

Chapter Seventeen

Betsy Jameson was sitting at the reception desk when I walked into Misty Ridge Catering with Jazzy in her pet carrier.

"I hope you don't mind," I said, tilting my head toward the carrier. "I always take Jazzy to work with me, and it's too warm today to leave her in the car while we talk."

"That's no problem whatsoever. I like cats." She gave me a tight smile. "You *will* leave her in the carrier, though, won't you? We have a kitchen in the back."

"Of course."

"Do take a seat."

I sat on one of the club chairs and placed Jazzy's carrier beside me. She meowed. Whether it was with approval or disdain was beyond me. Maybe it was apprehension. That's what I was feeling. Like Max, I didn't know if this woman wanted to make amends or trouble.

Betsy brought her tablet over and sat on the chair to my left. "Hello, kitty." She used a babytalk voice that would have made Max roll her eyes and grumble that Jasmine didn't appreciate that sort of behavior.

"I'd like to apologize for my friend, Maggie," I said. "She found Mr. Diggs's body at the masquerade ball, and she is desperate to find someone who saw something that can prove her innocence."

"I certainly understand her plight, but from what I've heard, nobody seemed to have been able to alibi anyone else to the authorities."

"That's right."

"Who told you about the food poisoning rumors?" she asked. "Are you or someone you know a member of the historical society?"

"Someone I know mentioned it to me—several people, as a matter of fact. I made many of the gowns for the masquerade ball."

"Oh, that's right." She leaned back in her chair and gave me a not-so-subtle appraising look. "Daddy said you had some sort of dress boutique."

"I design clothing from vintage patterns," I said.

"Right. Well. That must be fun."

"It is. It's also a lot of work." I inclined my head. "I'm sure you can identify."

"Sure." She smiled. "I'll have to stop in at your shop sometime."

"I'd appreciate that." I wished she'd get to the point she'd brought me here to make, but I reined in my impatience and waited to see what she'd say next.

"How do you know this…this woman who found Preston Diggs?"

"Maggie is the mother of my part-time assistant, Zoe."

She gave a slow nod. "And you're well acquainted with Maggie?"

"Not as much as I am with her daughter," I said. "Zoe is a wonderful young woman. In fact, she was responsible for making the masks to coordinate with the gowns I made for the ball."

"Interesting. Did she make a mask for Maggie?"

"The catering staff weren't wearing masks, but she made masks for my grandfather and me." I don't know why I'd felt inclined to say that. I always overshare when I'm nervous. I needed to simply hush and let Betsy give me a clue as to what I was actually doing here.

"Sounds like she's a very clever girl."

"She is."

Betsy picked up her tablet. "I'm sorry I'm chatting away like we have all the time in the world, and you told me you have plans this evening." She opened an app.

"Tell me how many people you plan on inviting to the event."

From that point on, Betsy Jameson was all business, and I still didn't know why she'd asked me to meet with her. Maybe after the food poisoning accusation, she was hard up for business. Or maybe I'd missed what she was after. Did she get it, or not?

I was driving back home when Detective Cranston called me. Since my phone was paired to my car, I was able to answer him handsfree.

"Hi, detective. How are you?"

"I've been busy asking those burning questions you had at lunchtime."

"Are you able to tell me anything?" I asked.

"Detective McAfee from the Brea Ridge Police Department will be in touch with you tonight or tomorrow. There was a mask outside the venue, and they want to see whether or not it's one of yours. I imagine you kept a record of who bought what dress and the coordinating mask?"

"Absolutely, but I'm not sure how that will help. Almost everybody there was wearing a mask."

"I know, but I've told him he can trust you, so he'll likely ask you other things as well," he said.

"Like what?"

"That's between the two of you."

I tried not to let my frustration show. "Is there anything you can tell me?"

"I can tell you it isn't likely Preston Diggs ingested poison. However, his autopsy showed upper airway edema and hyperinflated lungs suggestive of anaphylactic shock."

Gasping, I said, "So, the stabbing didn't kill him."

"Well, it didn't help and was indeed a contributing factor, but the stab wound and the anaphylaxis combined to do him in fairly quickly."

"Do you know what sort of allergy Mr. Diggs had?"

"Peanut," he said. "But I didn't tell you that."

"Okay. Thank you, Detective Cranston."

"You're welcome. McAfee is a good guy—you can trust him."

I took Jazzy home and fed her before getting ready for my date with Jason. I couldn't stop thinking about Preston Diggs's peanut allergy. His killer would have had to have known about the allergy, but I imagined that since Mr. Diggs was working in the food industry, his allergy would have been common knowledge among his staff and possibly his regular customers as well. However, Hot

Diggity hadn't been open for long. I wondered what Mr. Diggs had done prior to owning a restaurant. I never really knew anything about Tony's parents.

Jason arrived just after I finished getting ready. When I opened the door, he gave a low whistle that made me blush but that pleased me to no end.

We drove to a steakhouse in Bristol, and I was glad to be out of town. Away from Hot Diggity and Tony Diggs and Harry McCall and Betsy Jameson and Renata Crenshaw and anything that could interfere with our evening.

"How was your day?" I asked, as Jason was driving.

"Busy, but nice. Yours?"

"Busier than yesterday, interesting."

"Curious choice of words." He stopped for a red light and looked over at me. "What was so interesting about it?"

I pondered how much I wanted to tell him. I mean, I *wanted* to tell him everything—or most of it, with the exclusion of Max's input—but I didn't want it to spoil our time together.

The light turned, and Jason drove on. "You don't have to talk about it if you'd prefer not to."

"I want to give you the abridged version, if that's okay, and then I want us to let it go and not color our evening," I said. "Is that okay?"

"Works for me. Get it all out, and we'll toss it out the window."

"All right. I told you about the meeting with Betsy Jameson yesterday."

"Yes," he said, "and how Maggie angered the woman, and you had to leave."

"I should've known that wouldn't be the end of it, but I didn't expect Harry McCall to be on the porch of Shops on Main this morning shouting at me and threatening to ruin me. Grandpa came to see about me and then paid Mr. McCall a visit and said he'd bankroll my suit against him if he didn't stand down. Grandpa came back to tell me that, Monica saw him, and asked what he was doing there. We told her the whole story, and she said some women learn to stop being damsels in distress and take care of themselves. Then, when Grandpa and Monica went to lunch later, Max told—" Realizing what I'd said, I stopped speaking abruptly.

"Max told you what?" he asked.

I'd accidentally mentioned Max before, and Jason thought she was a client who came by the shop occasionally.

"Um…she saw them in the parking lot. She said Monica tried to take Grandpa's hand, but he wouldn't take it." I cleared my throat. "Then I had lunch with Detective Cranston and asked him about my theory on Mr. Diggs being poisoned. He wasn't, but the autopsy did show signs of anaphylaxis, and Detective McAfee from the Brea Ridge PD will be talking with me tonight or tomorrow. Then Betsy Jameson called and asked me if I'd come back and meet with her about Grandpa's party."

"Did you go?"

"Yes, and she acted as if it was just business, but I'm not sure it was." I decided not to tell him about Tony Diggs. Instead, I sank back against the seat and closed my eyes.

"And here I thought *I'd* had a busy day. Are you sure you're up for dinner?"

"Yes. Get me as far away from Abingdon as possible, just for a little while."

"As you wish." He grinned. "Damsel."

I laughed. "I can be a strong woman when I want to be."

"I believe you proved that already today."

"I did, didn't I? But it's nice to be a damsel sometimes too."

"I only hate I wasn't there to rescue you from Harry McCall," he said. "But I'm glad Dave was."

"Me, too." I paused. "I'd have handled it fine, but it was good for both of us, you know? It made Grandpa realize how much I still need him, even though I'm a grown woman, and it gave me the warm fuzzies that someone was willing to stand up for me."

He took my hand in his and raised it to his lips. "There's more than one person who'd fight a tiger for you, you know."

"I do know. And I'd do the same for them." I did hope I wouldn't have to, though, at least not tonight.

Chapter Eighteen

After my date with Jason, I was propped up in bed reading Victoria Holt's *Bride of Pendorric* when my phone buzzed. It was Max requesting a video chat.

When I opened the chat, I was surprised to find not only Max, but also Maggie on the call. Good thing I was wearing nice pajamas.

"Where are Dwight and Zoe?" I was trying to be flippant, as in, *why doesn't everyone call me for a chat at nearly midnight*, but Maggie took my question in stride.

"They're in bed. Look, I realize I messed up yesterday, and I'm sorry."

"It's okay."

"No, it isn't," she said. "I might've messed up a good lead for us."

I started to point out that alienating Betsy could turn out to be much worse for her than it would for me, but I decided not to mention it. Maggie already knew that very well. I only wish she'd have acted like it yesterday.

"I mentioned to Maggie that you met with your detective friend at lunch today," Max said. "Could he tell you anything useful?"

"Not until this afternoon, but he did learn that the autopsy suggested the possibility of anaphylaxis," I said. "Had Mr. Diggs ever informed the staff that he had any allergies?"

"Yes. He told every member of his staff as soon as they were hired that he had a severe peanut allergy. He required us all to scrub our hands and forearms as soon as we arrived at work before we put on our gloves." Maggie shook her head. "He said he knew many of us had children and that where there were children, there was peanut butter. I thought he was being overly cautious, but in light of his death, I guess not."

"Okay, so it sounds like Mr. Diggs's peanut allergy was common knowledge." I thought a second. "Did you see him eating anything at the ball? Maybe the killer tainted some food he ate."

"He was always tasting things to make sure they were satisfactory," Maggie said.

"Did you see anyone in particular handing him a food to try?" Max asked. "You know, like, *try this, Preston. There's not the first sign of a peanut in here.*"

"Nope. But, again, we were all swamped."

"Then let's talk about motive," I said. "What was his status—married, divorced, widowed, in a relationship?"

"He was a widower with a roving eye," Maggie said. "That's why he wanted the servers to bring pretty young—albeit not *too* young—women in to help serve at the masquerade ball. He said it was to charm the attendees, but I know better, especially given the way he treated Zoe."

"Let's narrow down the suspects." I held up my index finger. "You saw Tony and Harry McCall in close proximity to Mr. Diggs before he was stabbed." I raised an additional digit. "Detective Cranston said the Brea Ridge Police found a woman's mask outside the venue. I'm not sure why that's suspicious, given the number of masks floating around the fairgrounds that night, but Detective Cranston mentioned it."

"We need to find out how Junior felt about his dad," Max said. "He likes you, Amanda. Think you could wring a confession out of him?"

Lowering my hand, I said, "I seriously doubt it, but I'll reach out to him and see if he gives away any clues."

"What did Betsy say when you returned to her office today?" Maggie asked.

"Not a lot. I'm not quite sure why she asked me to come back and get the quote, unless she's really desperate for business. She did say she'd work up an estimate for Grandpa's party and email it to me tomorrow, but still—"

I frowned. "Something felt very off about our meeting. I wish there was something tangible I could grasp onto, but there isn't. It's only a feeling."

"Maggie, you should ask around among your fellow Hot Diggity workers to find out who Preston Diggs might have been seeing," Max said. "As the French say, *cherchez la femme.* I've been reading and watching a lot of stories and learned that the motive for murder is invariably love or money."

"Well, it's late," I said. "I need to get to sleep."

After we ended the call, I put a bookmark in *Bride of Pendorric*, placed it on the bedside table, and had little trouble falling asleep. I did, however, dream of masks, knives, and peanuts—giant grinning peanuts.

The next morning, I put on a pair of cuffed, wide-leg navy pants and a matching bolero jacket and felt ready to take on the world. That confidence lasted until I unlocked the door to Designs on You. Turns out it was false bravado. It would have been *real* bravado had I not been embroiled in a murder investigation and planning to meet with a detective—this one a stranger—again today.

"Good morning, darling," Max said, as I let Jazzy out of her carrier and got her food and water ready. "You look very Hepburn-esque."

"Katherine or Audrey?"

"Katherine. If you were going for Audrey, you'd have chosen cigarette pants."

I smiled, impressed with her eye for fashion. "Very good!"

There was a rap on the door before a large man stepped through the frame. The man, who resembled the actor, Shemar Moore, softly closed the door behind him and came on into the room.

"Good morning," he said.

"Hi." I realized I was standing there with my mouth slightly agape like a numbskull. "Welcome to Designs on You. How may I help you today?"

"I'm Detective McAfee with the Brea Ridge Police Department. Do you have time to answer a few questions?"

Max held out her wrists. "Handcuff me, handsome. I've been a bad, bad girl."

Oh, no. I couldn't concentrate on answering this man's questions if Max was in my head the whole time. "It might be better if we could speak in your office. I never know when someone is going to come in."

"Pooh. I'll behave. Just don't send the Adonis away."

"Or we *could* speak in the work area," I said. "I can put a note on each of the doors saying I'll return in half an hour and lock the doors."

"Do you mind?" he asked.

"Not at all." After I got the notes up and the doors locked, I sat down at the worktable and gestured for Detective McAfee to sit opposite me.

Max perched somewhere behind me so she could watch the dreamy detective.

Detective McAfee took out his phone and pulled up a photograph of a green and burgundy mask with black feathers. The photo was divided into two screens—one showing the front of the mask and the other showing the back.

I needed no more than a glance to tell the detective, "This mask came from the party supply store at the upper end of town. I saw a dozen like it when Zoe and I went there to get some ideas on what types of masks she'd like to make."

"You're sure?" he asked.

"You can go by there and see for yourself."

Returning the phone to his pocket, he said, "Great. That means any DNA we find on it would likely be inadmissible. The masks didn't happen to be individually packaged, did they?"

"I'm afraid not." When I saw that we both realized the mask was a dead end, I said, "I asked Maggie Flannagan if Preston Diggs ever mentioned having any sort of food allergy. She told me he informed all his employees of his life-threatening peanut allergy and gave them strict daily washing instructions when they were hired."

"Thanks. My partner has spoken with Ms. Flannagan and has found her to be defensive and argumentative, so I appreciate your passing along that information."

"I believe Maggie is terrified. Not because she's guilty of anything, but because she's a single mom who also cares for her elderly father. She's afraid she'll be framed for Mr. Diggs's murder because she was the one who found him."

"I understand her concerns," the detective said, "but she needs to talk with law enforcement the way she's talking with you if she wants us to help her."

"What if I could get her here? If I could get her to come to the shop and talk with you this morning, would you wait for her?"

"I will." He checked his watch. "That is, if she can get here in half an hour."

"Okay." I took out my phone and dialed Maggie's number.

Maggie answered on the first ring. "Amanda, is everything all right?"

"Everything is fine," I said. "I'm here with Detective McAfee of the Brea Ridge Police Department."

"And he's absolutely gorgeous and sweet as lemon pie," Max said.

Ignoring Max, I continued. "He's agreed to meet with you here at Designs on You if you can get here within half an hour. You and he can talk in the atelier, and I'll stay in the reception area. Maybe you won't be as nervous if you're here rather than in a police interrogation room."

"I would feel better in a more familiar environment," she said. "I'll be there in twenty minutes."

"I'll stay here with you the whole time, if you'd like," Max said.

"I'd rather you didn't—" Maggie began.

"Don't worry," I interrupted. "I won't listen in. It'll be just you and Detective McAfee. See you soon." I quickly ended the call. "Detective McAfee, would you like a cup of coffee while you wait?"

Chapter Nineteen

Detective McAfee and I were sitting in the reception room in the chairs by the window having coffee when Maggie arrived. I rose and unlocked the door for her. Since they were going to be talking in the atelier, I didn't lock the door back when I closed it.

Max had been staying true to her word and was behaving herself to the best of her ability. She had sung a verse or two of "Ain't Misbehavin'," but she sang softly and unobtrusively…for Max.

As Maggie and the detective walked into the workroom, I whispered, "I wish I could be a fly on the wall."

"I'll be your fly." She poked her head through the wall. "Good. Maggie has her back to me, so as long as

I'm quiet, she won't even know I'm here. Detective Dreamboat is showing Maggie the mask and asking her if she's seen it before. He's speaking kindly to her." She looked at me. "I'm not opposed to Maggie dating Ford if that should happen without any prompting, but I might be tempted to shove her in the yummy detective's direction if I knew whether or not he was single. Why don't you ask him?"

"I'm not asking him. That would be weird. Besides, I'm more concerned with getting Maggie exonerated. What's going on now?"

She peeped back into the room. "Maggie's telling him the mask looks familiar. She's positive she saw it the night of the ball. He asks if it's one her daughter made." She pulled her head out of the atelier and squinted at me. "Now, why would he ask her that if he already knows the answer? You've already told him where that mask came from."

"Maybe he's verifying that our stories remain the same."

"Oh." She put her head back through the wall. "Maggie said she's not familiar with every mask Zoe made, but she started putting a logo in her masks fairly early on. This mask doesn't have that logo. She's saying he could ask Zoe himself as long as she's allowed to stay with her daughter, who is a minor." She chuckled. "You go, Maggie! Oops."

"Oops, what?"

"Oops, she saw me and gave me the death glare," Max said. "That's what Zoe calls it. I see why now."

I huffed. "Now we won't know what's going on?"

"Yes, we will. Be quiet, and I'll listen. I'll just put my head a little ways into the wall." She listened for a moment. "He's telling her he doesn't need to talk with Zoe and that they're simply trying to identify the person who was wearing the mask because it was discarded at the back entrance of the exhibit hall. Maggie says that's the entrance the catering staff used. McAfee asks if any of the catering staff wore masks, and they didn't."

"It was my understanding that the people in the kitchen or food prep areas who wore masks were guests," I said.

"Yeah, according to Maggie, she recognized Renata Crenshaw even though she was wearing a mask because Preston Diggs addressed her by name. And she's telling him how she saw other people—either they lifted their masks or she identified them some other way, like Harry McCall and the scar on his chin—and later found out who they were through a photo of the historical society."

"Wow, she's really giving him some good information," I said.

Max nodded. "Yeah, she's telling him the others were Jill Eller and Norman something—she doesn't recall the surname."

She listened quietly for a moment, and Jazzy strolled over to lie on the floor and gaze up at her friend.

"McAfee is asking her about the argument she had with Diggs now," Max said after a moment. "He stressed that he isn't accusing her of anything, simply confirming that they did have an argument. Maggie asked him how he'd feel if he'd brought his daughter along to be an extra set of hands with pay—as his boss asked him to do—only to have to turn around and tell his daughter that she wouldn't be working after all because his jerk of a boss wanted hot young women and not jailbait to serve his food and entice partygoers to his new restaurant."

"Ooh. That's an excellent point, but it's gutsy. She's admitting she was furious with the victim," I said.

"Dreamboat says he'd be angry too, and then Maggie stepped up and said very quietly and with the great poise of an Englebright, 'But you wouldn't kill him. You'd tell him off and resolve to quit that stupid job as soon as you found another one. At least, that's what I did.'"

I was still leaning forward in my chair watching Max spy on Detective McAfee and Maggie when I heard footsteps in the hallway. I straightened and grabbed my sketchpad in an attempt to appear busy.

Sarah Conrad opened the door and came inside. "Hi, there."

"Hi, Sarah." I stood and placed the sketchpad on my desk. "How are you?"

"I'm fine. I've been upstairs meeting with Jason about the photos and saw your *Sale* sign." She cocked her head. "What is your cat so fascinated by on that wall?"

I glanced over to see Jazzy staring at Max who still had her head halfway through the wall. "Um…I believe she saw a bug over there a few minutes ago."

"What kind of bug?" Max asked.

"A ladybug," I said.

"All right," Max said. "You'd better be glad you didn't call me a cockroach or a pill bug."

"Aw, that's sweet. She's a beautiful cat," Sarah said.

"Thank you." I gave her a bright smile. "What poses did you decide to go with?"

Sarah took out her phone and showed me the four photos she'd decided to get made into various sizes.

I gazed down at Joey's wide grin featuring a permanent tooth that was still coming in. The child held a ferret in each arm. "Joey has grown so much even in the time I've known him."

"They do that, I'm afraid. It seems as if you blink, and they're another year older. You'll see one of these days."

I remembered the book I'd bought him and got it off my desk. "If you'll remember, I promised him a new book for helping me wrangle Biscuit the other day."

Shaking her head, Sarah said, "I still don't know why you promised him a new book. Biscuit is his responsibility after all."

"I know, but he's such a sweetheart, and I love encouraging kids to read every chance I get."

"You're sweet. Thank you." She started to look at the clearance rack but turned back. "Before I get caught up in looking at all your pretty clothes, let me tell you this. I heard something really interesting in my knitting circle yesterday."

"I'm all ears," I said.

"Guess who Preston Diggs was dating last year?" Without giving me time to hazard a guess, she went on. "Betsy Jameson of Misty Ridge Catering. That's how he knew about the food poisoning allegations. Can you believe it?"

My jaw dropped. "Are you serious?"

Sarah nodded. "I was shocked too. What a creep he must've been to do an ex-girlfriend that way just to get ahead."

I gave Max a saucer-eyed stare as Sarah went to browse. I mouthed, *Did you hear that*?

Almost immediately after Sarah paid for her new shirtdress and left, Detective McAfee and Maggie came out of the atelier.

"Ms. Tucker, thank you for your time and for the use of your workroom. I appreciate your assistance." He nodded at Maggie. "Ms. Flannagan, if there's anything else you can think of, please let me know."

"Yes, sir. I have your card."

The detective left, and Maggie slouched onto one of the chairs by the window.

"Is he gone?" she asked.

"Yes. You saw him leave," I said.

"I mean completely. Off the porch and everything."

"I'll check," Max said. "I'm not opposed to watching that man walk away." She hurried through the wall and out onto the porch.

"Do you need some water or coffee?" I asked Maggie.

She shook her head. "No, thank you. I'm fine."

"Are you feeling any better after talking with Detective McAfee?" I sat on the other chair by the window.

"I am. I think I'm less of a suspect now. I know I'm not entirely out of the woods, but I don't think I'm the only person on their radar either."

Max came back inside. "Detective Dreamboat is in his car trying to ease into traffic. I don't know why. If I had a siren on my car, I'd turn it on and whip out, daring anyone to hit me."

"Have you ever driven a car, Aunt Max?" Maggie asked.

"I most certainly have. I once drove a Model A Ford. Dot said it was the most frightened she'd ever been in her life." She smiled. "I thought it was exhilarating."

"I can imagine," I said. "I heard an interesting piece of news while you were talking to the detective."

"Really?" Maggie folded her arms. "I'd have thought you and Aunt Max were too busy with the play-by-play of my conversation to do anything else."

"Yeah. Sorry about that." I grimaced. "Did you get distracted?"

"Not overmuch. I live with my teenaged daughter and elderly father. I'm well versed in tuning out annoyances."

"Ouch," Max said. "And since Amanda is the one who said she wished she could be a fly on the wall—thus, putting me up to mischief—I'm going to tell the secret. Preston Diggs used to date Betsy Jameson. That's how he knew about the food poisoning."

Maggie looked at me. "Why didn't you tell that to McAfee before he left? That's an excellent motive for murder right there."

"It is, if it's true. I need to verify the information before I pass it along."

Chapter Twenty

Unfortunately, the best way I knew to get the real story of any Betsy Jameson– Preston Diggs romance was to ask Tony Diggs. So, that's what I did.

Although I didn't have a phone number for Tony, it wasn't hard to find him on social media. I sent him a direct message saying:

Hi, Tony. I'm concerned about you. I know how hard it must be dealing with your father's death. If you want to talk, I'm here.

"And now we wait," I said to Maggie and Max.

We didn't have to wait long.

It's terrible, he responded. *I feel so alone. I lost my mother a few years ago, you know. And now Dad is gone too. I wish I had someone I could pour out my feelings to.*

"Manipulative much?" Maggie rolled her eyes.

Max pretended to play the violin. "He didn't seem all that shaken when he was here trying to get you to have dinner with him yesterday."

"You hardhearted women."

Would you like to meet at the sports bar for a drink? I typed. *I could meet you there after work.*

I'd like that very much, he said. *I'll be there at five o'clock.*

See you then, I said.

I logged off the social media site and shut my laptop.

"What will Jason say about your agreeing to meet Tony Diggs for a drink after work?" Maggie asked.

"He'll be fine with it," I said. "He's working this evening, so we don't have plans. But, even if we did, he knows how important it is to me to help you clear your name."

"Why?" Maggie asked. "I've never gone out of my way to be nice to you."

"Maybe not, but I consider Max, Zoe, and Dwight to be family," I said, "and you're *their* family. Family helps family."

"I appreciate that. I appreciate *you*." She grabbed her purse. "I'd better go. Thanks for letting me and the detective use your workshop." She ducked her head and went out the door.

"She's not good with emotions," Max said.

"I've noticed."

"Hopefully, we can help her get better with them." She wandered over to the window and watched Maggie leave before turning her attention back to me. "As for you, young lady—"

"Uh-oh."

"—whatever you do, don't go to any secondary locations with Tony Diggs. I saw it on a TV show or read it in a book or something that it's dangerous to go to a secondary location with a stranger. That's where they kill you."

"Thanks for the advice, but I will definitely *not* be going anywhere with Tony. Plus, I plan on leaving Jazzy here at Shops on Main while I'm having that drink, so you'll know if I don't come back in a timely manner and can call and check on me."

"Believe you me, I'll do it. While you're gone, I'll read our book to Jasmine because she's in the book club too, you know."

Jazzy's tail swished at the sound of her name.

"Naturally," I said.

"You can see how excited she is." Max went over to the cat and waved her hand.

The tabby rolled onto her back and batted at Max's hand with her paws, and I wondered if the day would drag or fly by as I waited for my meeting with Tony. It went by far too quickly.

I was hoping to get to the sports bar before Tony so I could choose where we sat. No such luck. When I arrived, he was sitting at a pub table in an ill-lit back corner of the restaurant and was facing the door.

Raising my hand in greeting, I wound through the tables to the bar where I asked for a diet soda before sitting across from Tony, who was halfway through a beer.

"If I get sloshed, will you drive me home?" he asked.

"I can't. I have to go back to work. I'd be glad to use my app to get you a ride, though."

"Gee, thanks," he said. "You're all heart. Why are you going back to work? The masquerade ball is over."

"For now. The rescheduling is in full swing from what I hear. Besides, I have to replenish stock I sold out of while I was making ballgowns." While what I'd told Tony was misleading, I hadn't technically lied. I *did* need to replenish stock, and I *was* returning to work. I could have simply told him no, I didn't want to drive him to a secondary location; but I felt that would have sounded rude, and I needed him to give me information about his father and Betsy Jameson.

"Are you hungry?" he asked.

"I wouldn't mind a little something."

When the waiter brought my soda, we ordered a basket of chips.

"How are you holding up?" I asked softly after the waiter had left.

"I'm as good as could be expected. I mean, I don't feel as if I've had time to truly process everything yet. I've been dealing with the funeral arrangements, figuring out what's what with the restaurant, filing insurance claims, all that stuff."

"Do you plan to reopen the restaurant?"

"I don't know," Tony said. "It was Dad's place. Without him, I don't know that I even want to keep it. I've already had a couple of offers on it, so I might sell."

"You've had offers on Hot Diggity already? That seems awfully intrusive and cold."

He shrugged. "Business is business, I guess. Someone sees an opportunity and wants to be first in line. It's crazy. One of the offers was from Betsy Jameson."

That was the perfect opening for my questions.

"Betsy Jameson? That's surprising," I said. "I mean, I heard she and your father used to date. Wouldn't buying his restaurant be a painful reminder for her? Or do you imagine she'd like to take over the restaurant in order to honor him in some way?"

Tony gave a bitter bark of laughter. "Trust me when I tell you there wasn't any love lost between my dad and Betsy Jameson. Dad was an old player. He'd see Betsy one night, Renata the next, and somebody else the night after that."

"Renata? Renata Crenshaw?"

"Yeah, he saw her a few times. He joked that she was a little old for his taste, but she had connections."

"What about Betsy?"

"They got along well as far as I know—that is, until she found out about his other girlfriends." He snorted. "Betsy thought she was going to become Mrs. Preston Diggs, but Dad didn't play that game. He loved one woman enough to marry her—my mother. These other women were just people to pass the time with. He wasn't serious about any of them."

The waiter brought our chips, another beer for Tony, and another soda for me. We thanked him, and he discreetly left us to our conversation.

I was eager to keep Tony on the subject of Betsy and the other women his father had dated. "I imagine Betsy stopped seeing him after she learned she wasn't the only contender for his affections."

"Oh, yeah. She blew up on him big time at a restaurant in Bristol. I'm surprised you didn't hear about it."

"I didn't hear a thing."

"That's how she found out he was seeing someone else," he said. "Dad said she acted like a crazy person. Security had to make her leave, and the restaurant threatened to call the police on her."

"How embarrassing. How long did they date?"

"Several months."

I grinned and leaned forward, hoping to appear approving of his father's actions. "Is that why he told Renata about the food poisoning incident—to get back at her for embarrassing him in the restaurant? Or did Renata find out after hiring Misty Ridge Catering that your dad had gone out with Betsy and used the food poisoning claim as an excuse to fire her?"

"At first, Renata didn't know anything about Dad's relationship with Betsy. I doubt she'd have cared either way. Dad swooped in and took that catering job from Misty Ridge because he wanted it. Plus, like you said, it showed her she couldn't embarrass Preston Diggs in public and get away with it."

Sipping my soda, I nodded in apparent agreement. "It sounds as if the person she ultimately humiliated was herself. But wasn't your dad concerned when Harry McCall threatened to sue him for slander or libel? I mean, McCall has a reputation for being a tough lawyer."

"It was slander. Dad told Renata about the food poisoning. McCall was going to sue the historical society for libel because they published the story in their newsletter." He swigged his beer. "Dad wasn't scared of Harry McCall for one millisecond though. He had dirt on that old man too."

I felt my eyebrows nearly hit my hairline. "Dirt? What kind of dirt?"

Tony shrugged. "I don't know. Dirt people didn't want others to know. Dad had sensitive information about lots of powerful people. I hope I can find a notebook or something that spells it all out for me when I go through Dad's office."

"It does sound like valuable information to have." I didn't really believe that, but the man was staring at me and expecting a response.

"You bet it's valuable. You know what they say, knowledge is power."

"Knowledge can also be dangerous," I said, feeling it overkill to remind Tony that it could have been that knowledge that got his father killed.

Chapter Twenty-One

When I got back to Shops on Main, Grandpa's pickup truck was in the parking lot. I'd given him copies of my keys after I leased the shop.

I hurried inside to find him sitting on my desk chair with Jazzy on his lap listening to Max read from the tablet.

"Oh, hi," Max said. "I'm slipping. I didn't even hear you arrive."

"You were too absorbed in your book," Grandpa said.

I went around the side of the desk to give him a peck on the cheek. "This is a nice surprise."

"I was a little worried about you being out with that dodgy Tony." Max waved her hand, and her tablet shut off. "I don't trust that wannabe cake eater as far as I could throw him, so I called Dave. He volunteered to come and wait with Jasmine and me."

"How did your talk over drinks go?" Grandpa rubbed Jazzy under her chin, and the cat purred loudly.

Sitting down on one of the chairs by the window and taking off my shoes, I said, "Very productive. Not only had Preston Diggs been dating Betsy Jameson, but he also dated Renata Crenshaw."

"So, Tony's pop really *was* a cake eater!" Max exclaimed.

"If by *cake eater*, you mean a ladies' man—" I was pretty sure I had Max's meaning correct—"then he apparently was. And when I asked Tony if his dad was concerned about Harry McCall's threat to sue him, Tony said his dad wasn't scared of Harry because he had some dirt on him."

Max moved closer. "What was it? I want to know."

"Tony didn't say, and I don't believe he knew," I said. "He thinks his dad kept a notebook or a file or something with information that, according to Tony, could be used to blackmail a lot of powerful people. He's hoping to find it among his dad's belongings."

Insistent as ever, Max asked, "Who *are* these people, and what secrets are they trying to keep hidden?"

"He didn't know. He was still trying to find out himself."

"I wish I could see that notebook or whatever Preston Diggs kept his juicy information squirreled away in," Max said.

"Me, too," Grandpa said. "It would certainly provide a list of people who had more motive to murder Preston Diggs than Maggie had."

"Oh, yeah." Max nodded at him. "That would also be helpful."

"Also?" I asked. "You're just being nosy!"

"No, I'm not!" She pressed her lips together. "Okay, I am, but some of that stuff might be really good to know. Say old Sally Sweet popped her husband for the insurance money, and then she wanders into Designs on You one day and asks you to make her an outfit."

"To wear to the funeral, no doubt." Grandpa grinned.

"Sure. Why not? She wants to look nice. Anyway, would you do it? Would you make her an outfit if you knew she was a killer?"

"I'd *have* to, wouldn't I?"

"And run the risk of her coming back here and knocking you off if she decided she didn't like her dress?" Max asked.

"Would you rather she pop me because I refused to make her an outfit in the first place?"

Max frowned. "That's a valid argument. We'd best steer clear of Sally Sweet."

Rubbing my temples with both hands, I asked, "Could we please get back on track?"

"Of course." Max shrugged. "You're the one who brought up the potential blackmail material. I was simply weighing out how that information could benefit us."

Grandpa chuckled. "Did you learn anything else from Tony Diggs that might prove useful?"

"Yes. Tony is considering selling Hot Diggity and has already received three offers on it—one offer is from Betsy Jameson."

"Ooh!" Max brought her hands up to her throat. "Do you think she wants to buy the joint to burn it to the ground because that man did her wrong?"

"I highly doubt it," I said. "I feel it's more likely she wants an established restaurant she could easily move into."

"I agree," Grandpa said. "For someone with restaurant knowledge, Hot Diggity would be an excellent deal if the price was right. It's in a good location, has brand new equipment, is fully staffed, and has vendors already in place."

"How about you then, Dave? You can cook—and well, from what I've seen. Why don't you buy the restaurant?"

I knew what Max was doing, and I appreciated it. However, I also knew there was no way Grandpa would buy a restaurant. Then again, I *knew* he'd never leave Abingdon, and here he was considering doing just that.

"I'm too old to take on an endeavor of that magnitude," he said.

"It's getting late. Don't you and Monica have plans this evening?" I kept my tone light, trying not to betray the fact that I was dying to know if he was any closer to making a decision about leaving us for Nebraska.

"Nope. Not today."

I glanced at Max.

"Why not?" She sat on the desk and peered at Grandpa. "Have you seen her true colors at last?"

"Monica is a wonderful woman," he said.

"It looked to me like you were angry with her yesterday in the parking lot when you two were on your way to lunch." She raised her chin. "Don't try to give me any hokum, Dave Tucker."

"I wouldn't dream of it." He smiled slightly. "As a matter of fact, I *was* irritated with Monica because, in my opinion, she treated Amanda unfairly. I let her know without any room for misinterpretation that nothing and no one comes before my family and especially not before my granddaughter."

"Does that mean you're staying in Abingdon with us?" Max clapped her hands. "Yay!"

"That's not what I said."

"Grandpa, Jason passed along a great piece of advice that his grandmother gave him. She said, 'Don't do anything rash. Go to this new place for a week or two if you want to, but don't sell out and move. Don't make any snap decisions and do something you'll regret.'"

"She told him exactly that, did she?" He arched an eyebrow.

"Yes!" Max said. "I heard him tell Amanda myself."

He looked at his watch. "I'd better get going, and I'm positive Jazzy knows it's past her suppertime." He plucked the cat off his lap and placed her gently onto the floor.

"Yeah, I need to go home as well."

Max hopped off the desk. "Well, why don't all of you just breeze and leave me here all alone?"

"I'm sorry, but I am pretty tired," I said. "I'll talk with both of you soon."

Grandpa gave me a hug and winked at Max before he left.

"He appeared to be lost in thought as he walked out," I said, as I retrieved Jazzy's carrier. I watched him striding across the parking lot with his phone in his hand. "Wonder who he's calling?"

"I hope he's calling that blasted Monica to tell her he's staying in Abingdon," Max said. "With both of us putting the screws to him—you with that 'don't sell out' work around and me with the hard sell—we've convinced him not to go."

I nodded to placate Max, but I wasn't convinced in the least that Grandpa had made up his mind to stay. Plus, I knew Grandpa. There was something he was determined to fix. I'd seen it on his face just before he stepped out of the shop. He got that same look on his face when something needed "tending to," be it a leaky faucet or a sticky situation. But going to Nebraska—or not—wasn't the situation on his mind this evening. It was something else—that much I knew. But what it *was*? That, I had no idea about.

Chapter Twenty-Two

Knowing from the weeks of tedious work on her ballgown that Renata Crenshaw was an early riser, I called her from work first thing Thursday morning.

My name apparently came up on her phone because she answered with, "Having another sale already?"

"No," I said. "I'm merely calling to see how you're doing."

"That's kind of you. I'm well and plans for the masquerade ball are back on track."

"Wonderful. I'm happy the historical society's fundraiser will take place after all."

"So am I, dear. So am I."

"But *you*, Ms. Crenshaw. Are you okay? I had no idea you and Preston Diggs had a relationship."

There was such a long silence on the line that I was beginning to be afraid Ms. Crenshaw and I had been disconnected. I opened my mouth to ask if she was still there, but she began to speak.

"Who told you that nonsense?"

"Tony, Mr. Diggs's son. We went to school together, so we've known each other for ages." Not well, but I didn't think a lengthy explanation was in order.

She harumphed. "Since the young man is grieving, I can forgive his overinflated perception of my so-called relationship with his father. Preston and I were acquaintances, nothing more. We shared a meal from time to time to discuss historical society business, but I do that with many of our members. As the president, I need to be kept well informed."

"Of course, you do. I'm sorry if I offended you."

"Not at all." She sounded really offended. "I simply didn't want you to have the wrong impression about Preston Diggs and me."

Unable to come up with a response to that statement, I said, "Well, I certainly am glad things are moving along on rescheduling the ball. Maybe Misty Ridge would be willing to cater."

"Why on earth would you think I'd even *consider* hiring Betsy Jameson? I've already fired her once."

"Oh, but I—"

"You what?" she demanded.

"I thought maybe Mr. Diggs had…um…misrepresented Misty Ridge Catering in the whole food poisoning story. After all, Mr. McCall was threatening to sue him for slander." *And you for libel*, I added in my head.

"You're making a number of suppositions about people and things you know nothing about, young lady. I've wasted enough time on this call. Good day." She hung up.

I put down my phone and turned to see Max lying on the floor beside Jazzy.

"There went *that* customer," I said.

"Who cares? The only glad rags you were ever going to sell her were the masquerade gown that her nitpickiness made you spend far too much time on and that shirtdress that—even though it was already on sale—she made you knock an extra ten percent off of."

"That's true. Still, I don't want her bad-mouthing me all over town."

Max scoffed. "Like anybody would give two hoots about her opinion. Who do you believe about her relationship with Preston Diggs—her or Tony?"

"Tony. He had no reason to lie to me. I got the impression Renata Crenshaw was embarrassed."

"Or hiding something." She raised herself up off the floor, and she and Jazzy came over to my chair. "You know I don't hold that Tony guy in high regard whatsoever, but I don't get the impression he's crafty enough to tell you lies about his dad in order to divert suspicion onto someone else."

I picked up Jazzy and gave her a snuggle. "Me, either. And for Renata Crenshaw to get angry enough to hang up on me? That sends up a lot of red flags."

It wasn't but a few minutes later that Betsy Jameson strolled into Designs on You.

"Gee, what is this?" Max asked. "Preston Diggs's Broken Hearts Club Day?"

"Betsy, hi." I sat Jazzy onto the floor and rose to greet the woman. "This is a nice surprise."

"I was planning to email you a quote for your grandfather's party when I got to work, but then I realized I was driving right by here." She smiled and looked around the shop. "You've got some lovely things here."

"Thank you." I offered her a cup of coffee, but she declined.

After she'd wandered around the shop for a moment, she came back to sit on a chair in front of my desk.

I took a seat behind the desk and asked, “What’s the verdict?”

Betsy took her tablet from her tote bag, opened the tablet, and turned it where I could also see the screen. She went over the various options and the prices.

“Applesauce!” Max exclaimed, looking at the quote from over my shoulder. “Who are we inviting—the entire National Guard with the Canadian Mounted Police thrown in for good measure?”

While I didn’t voice my opinion to Betsy Jameson, I agreed with Max. Those prices appeared to be terribly steep. “Thank you. If you’ll send a copy to my email address, I can print it out and give it further consideration.”

“All right. Only please don’t share this quote with anyone else. I gave you a deal because we got off to such a rocky start.”

“A *deal*?” Max threw her hands up in the air. “Cleopatra in a pickup truck! I’d hate to see what she’d charge someone who didn’t get the enemies and family discount.”

Before I could suppress it, a giggle escaped me. “That’s all water under the bridge.”

Betsy probably thought I was insane, but I was used to that by now.

“Will you continue your catering business if you end up buying Hot Diggity?” I asked.

Eyes widening, Betsy asked, “What makes you think I want to buy a restaurant?”

“Tony Diggs mentioned that you’d put in an offer on his father’s restaurant.”

Her face reddened. “His father’s restaurant.” Her voice was scornful and bitter. “It was supposed to have been *our* restaurant. I imagine Tony left out that bit of information.”

For the second time already that morning, I was at a loss for words. Luckily for me, Betsy didn’t wait for my response.

“He and I had made big plans together, or so I thought. We were going to open the restaurant and work side by side.” Her eyes filled with tears.

I opened my middle desk drawer, removed a pack of tissues, and slid them over to her.

She removed one from the packet and dabbed at her eyes. “It was all a lie—at least, on his part. To him, I was one among many. His betrayal might have hurt me even more than my ex-husband’s did. I thought Preston was my second chance at happiness, that we were building something special together.”

“I’m so sorry.”

Betsy continued as if I hadn’t spoken. I wasn’t sure she’d even heard me.

“Not only did he go ahead and open the restaurant without me, he tried to take the one thing I had left by dragging the reputation of my catering business through the mud." She shook her head. "I still can't understand why he'd do that. He'd already hurt me so much. Why did he have to drive the stake into my heart even deeper?"

After wiping her eyes with the tissue again, she stood and attempted to smile. "I apologize for going off on that tangent. I need to get to work. Please let me know if you have any questions about the quote."

"I will. Thank you."

"Well, I'm fairly sure Betsy's dad killed Preston Diggs now," Max said, as Betsy pulled the door closed behind her.

"What makes you think so?" I asked softly.

"If you were her dad, wouldn't *you* have wanted to kill the creep?"

Chapter Twenty-Three

A couple of hours later, Connie brought a vase filled with white, yellow, and pink roses into the reception area.

"Connie, those are gorgeous," I said.

"I think so too." She smiled. "They're for you—delivered to Delightful Home by mistake. They came a few minutes ago, but I was waiting for your customer to leave before I brought them over."

My heart lifted. *Jason. He knows how much pressure I've been under lately, and he's sent me a pick-me-up.*

Grinning and blushing like a schoolgirl, I took the flowers from Connie and placed them on my desk. I opened the card.

My heart plummeted.

Thanks for everything. You're the best. Love, Tony

Tony. Not Jason.

"Oh." That syllable told Connie all she needed to know.

"Aw, sweetie, I'm sorry."

"It's okay," I said. "I thought they were probably from Jason, but instead they're from Tony Diggs. I had a drink with him last night because I know how devastated he must be over his father's death."

"I…um…I saw Betsy leaving here earlier. I was going to say hello, but she seemed upset and hurried out the door before I could get her attention."

"She came by to give me the quote for a party I'm considering having." I didn't fill Connie in on any of the details as they weren't relevant to what had upset Betsy. "We talked about her relationship with Preston Diggs."

"The man who was murdered at the masquerade ball?" she asked.

"Yes. Tony—" I jabbed my thumb in the direction of the flowers. "—is his son. He told me that Betsy and his father had dated. For Betsy, it was serious."

"I'm guessing that for Mr. Diggs, it was not."

"Right. Anyway, Tony told me that his father had compromising information on a lot of people, including Betsy's dad. I wish I'd thought to ask her if she knew anything about where Preston kept his sensitive information. So far, Tony hasn't been able to find it."

"Is he *sure* it even exists?" She rubbed her chin. "Maybe Mr. Diggs told his son he had all this blackmail material in order to impress him."

"I hope that's all it is. I shudder to think of all the lives Tony Diggs would happily destroy for no reason other than to prove he really could." I hoped I wasn't painting an unfair picture of Tony for Connie. After all, I hadn't known Tony since middle school, and I hadn't truly known him then. But simply based on what I'd seen of him this past week, I got the impression that any power whatsoever would go straight to his head.

"I'm going to call Betsy and check on her. I'll ask her in a roundabout way—or, heck, I might just come out and ask—if she knows whether or not Preston Diggs had notes or files or whatever on some of the more influential people in town."

"Thanks," I said.

"I'll let you know what I find out."

"You think Betsy will tell her?"

I started at the sound of Max's voice. She'd been in the atelier reading while I sat at my desk fine-tuning the detailing I wanted on my 1930s' suit jacket. I waited until I was sure Connie was back across the hall at Delightful Home before answering Max.

"I hope she will."

"Poor Betsy. I almost feel badly enough for her to encourage you to let her cater a party for Dave."

"Me too. But pitying someone and having scads of extra money are two different things," I said. "Besides, I hope there's no reason to throw Grandpa a party."

Connie came back a short while later to report that Betsy did think Preston Diggs knew some secrets people would prefer he didn't.

"For example, he once threatened to 'let it slip' that her dad had been involved in a shady estate deal."

"What kind of shady deal?" Max asked.

"What was shady about it?" I asked Connie.

"Well, according to Betsy, it was innocent enough—one of Mr. McCall's clients left him the bulk of her estate. But Mr. Diggs contended that he had proof that Mr. McCall had coerced the client in some way."

"But how could he prove that?" I asked. "Did he have a letter from Mr. McCall saying, 'Ha! Ha! Tricked you!'?"

Connie chuckled. "I thought it sounded a little hokey myself. And knowing Betsy, I asked her if she didn't think this fellow was gaslighting her. Of course, she didn't. She believed every word he said, even after she caught him with someone else."

"She must have been so enamored of him."

Detective Cranston stopped in, saw Connie, and said, "Don't mind me. I'm scoping out the sale for my wife."

"I'd better get back to Delightful Home." She smiled and nodded at Detective Cranston. "Good luck finding something."

"I'm not shopping," Detective Cranston said once Connie had left.

"I didn't think you were."

"I came to warn you."

My eyes widened. "Against what?"

"Tony Diggs was arrested on a drunk and disorderly conduct charge early this morning. He's being held in jail until he's sober, and then he'll be released with a summons. I wanted to let you know because he was talking about you—or, rather, yelling about you—when the officers brought him in."

"Yelling what?"

"He said his dad had some secrets on a lot of powerful people and that he told you all about it over dinner last night."

"We didn't have dinner," I quickly interjected. "We had a drink over chips. I met with him because he seemed so distraught over the death of his father."

"Either way, he said you were privy to this information and that you wouldn't let anything happen to him."

"I'm not privy to anything. I mean, yes, he told me Mr. Diggs had some incriminating information on some people, but he included that he—Tony—doesn't know where it's at. He's in the process of trying to find it."

Detective Cranston spread his hands. "Well, he even called out to Harry McCall, who was there visiting a client, that his dad knew what Harry had done and that soon everyone would know. I simply wanted to warn you that Tony might come here looking for you when he gets out of jail, especially if he thinks there was more to your having a drink with him than just your comforting a grieving friend."

"Thank you."

"You're welcome," he said. "Don't hesitate to call me if he comes by and frightens you or won't leave."

I was finishing up with a couple of customers who were buying short sets when Monica came into the shop.

"Hi, Monica. I'll be with you in a few minutes."

"Take your time," she said. "No rush." She sat on one of the navy chairs by the window and called Jazzy.

Jazzy didn't come. She was busy being entertained by Max, who stuck her tongue out at Monica and continued to mesmerize Jazzy by waving her hands around.

When my customers left, I joined Monica by the window and sat on the chair beside the one she was in.

"How are you?" I asked.

"I'm fine. I'm leaving early today, but I simply had to come apologize to you."

"For what?"

"Dave made me realize how unkind I've been to you lately," she said. "I convinced him that he sometimes needs to allow you to stand on your own two feet and be an independent young woman, but I admitted to being a teensy bit jealous of the close relationship the two of you have."

"I adore my grandpa. And while I feel I am absolutely an independent person, I don't see anything wrong with families leaning on each other. In fact, I believe that's what families are for."

"I agree, and since you and I are going to be family too, I hope we can let bygones be bygones and get along well."

I managed to smile and say something nice but noncommittal to Monica, and she finally left.

Looking at Max, I asked, "Do you think this means Grandpa is going to Nebraska with her?"

"I think it means I need to step up my haunting."

"What good would that do?"

"It'd make me feel better," she said.

Chapter Twenty-Four

I was determined to finish cutting out the pattern for the suit I'd been working on before I left work. Max and I were in the atelier. She was reading on her tablet, sometimes aloud to me, while I pinned the pattern to the gray worsted wool.

Hearing someone come in the reception door, I called, "Be right with you!"

Max floated over to the doorway to see who was there. "It's—"

Before she could finish, Harry McCall burst into the atelier.

"Mr. McCall." I was startled and a little frightened, but I managed to keep my composure. "I beg your pardon, but could you please wait for me in the reception area? I'll be there in a moment."

"No, I will not wait."

"Look, if you're still upset over the incident between Betsy and me, you're wasting your time. She and I are fine now. She stopped by this morning with a quote for my grandfather's party."

"You and she are fine now, are you?" He scoffed. "You want to pretend all is well while you and your boyfriend conspire to ruin our family."

I squinted at him. "Why would Jason and I want to hurt you?"

"Don't play dumb. I know you're involved with Tony Diggs. He's a rotten apple that didn't fall far from the bitter, slimy tree on which it was grown."

"I'm not involved with Tony. I know him from school but only marginally."

"Tony told me at the jail that you and he know what I'd done. What did he mean by that, Ms. Tucker?" he asked.

"I'm not sure, but according to Betsy, Tony could be talking about the estate your client gifted you. Although Tony seems to believe the client was coerced, Betsy cleared all that up." I hoped that would be enough to satisfy this man, who was staring at me as if he'd lost all vestiges of rational thought. What a time to have left my phone in the reception area.

"Tony said he had proof." He advanced toward me, further hemming me between himself and the door. "Tell me what proof Tony has and where he's keeping it."

"I don't know." I backed up until my legs were against the worktable.

"Liar!"

"Detective Cranston is on his way." Max came to put herself between Harry McCall and me. I appreciated the support but knew there was nothing more she could do to help. Still, I was relieved to know Cranston was on his way.

"Why are you worried?" I asked Mr. McCall. "Betsy said Tony's allegations were false."

"Even so, it would look bad if Tony made public whatever he's calling evidence. At the time that generous gift was made, I had a gambling addiction and was in a lot of debt. I was on the verge of bankruptcy. Any hint of suspicion that I somehow manipulated my client into gifting me that much-needed bequest might open me up to an ethics investigation and ruin my business."

"If you're innocent, you'll be able to prove that. Right?"

Mr. McCall clenched his fists. "Preston Diggs was a piece of garbage who deserved to die! He broke my daughter's heart and then destroyed the reputation of her catering company. I don't blame her for putting ground peanuts in the idiot's Bearnaise sauce!" His eyes widened as he realized he'd gone too far in his rant.

Looking around wildly, his eyes landed on the sewing table to his right. He grabbed a pair of my scissors.

I could feel my heart pounding in my throat. This man was going to stab me. With my favorite scissors.

Realizing Max had left the atelier, I heard her screaming, "Hurry! Hurry!"

Unfortunately, unless Grandpa, Dwight, Zoe, or Maggie was there, I was the only one who could hear her.

"Please put those scissors down," I said. "I understand how you feel, but this is not the answer. How did you know Betsy put peanuts into Mr. Diggs's Bearnaise sauce? Did she do it to make it taste funny, not knowing he had an allergy?"

"I saw her do it. I thought it was poison, but it wasn't. I should've known better. Betsy would never have done anything to hurt all those people."

"I know she wouldn't. She's a great person." *A great person who put ground peanuts in the food of a man deathly allergic to them.*

"Still, I didn't know. I knew he'd pushed her to her limit—that maybe he'd shoved her over the edge," he muttered.

I wasn't sure he was even aware of me at that moment, and I was glad of it, except that he still had my favorite scissors and was brandishing them like a weapon.

"I thought maybe she'd poisoned the sauce to make Preston sick—to pay him back a little for the way he'd treated her."

That would do it. "Who could blame her? And who could blame you if you stabbed Mr. Diggs to contaminate the investigation?"

He nodded. "Fatally harming Preston Diggs was never my or Betsy's intention."

"I believe a jury will take all the circumstances under consideration when they hear the testimony—"

He barked out a humorless laugh. "What we did will never go before a jury."

I gulped. "No. Of course, it won't. I'm certainly not going to tell anyone. But please put down my scissors. You're scaring me." I thought of something else that might convince him I was on his side but just needed a little favor from him. "I would love it, though, if you could advise Maggie Flannagan on how to avoid being arrested for Mr. Diggs's murder."

"She avoids it like everyone else—she keeps her mouth shut."

"Good advice. Thank you."

"But I'm afraid I can't trust you to keep your mouth shut, Ms. Tucker. You and your boyfriend are too greedy to do that."

"No, I'm—"

The building alarm started blaring.

Harry McCall raised the scissors over his head, and I caught his arm with both hands and began kicking him with my right leg.

Everything was a blur until Detective Cranston came running into the atelier and grabbed Harry McCall, pulling his arms behind his back. I looked down and saw the scissors in my own left hand—I'd managed to wrestle them away from my attacker.

"Thank you," I said, as I slumped onto a chair.

Detective Cranston said, "You're welcome."

I genuinely appreciated his help as well, but I was looking at Max when I spoke.

She grinned and winked. "Sorry it took me so long to make that stupid alarm go off again."

That evening after I'd given my statement to the police, Detective Cranston drove me back to Shops on Main so I could pick up my car. Noticing the lights were on in my shop and that Grandpa's truck was in the parking lot, I told Detective Cranston I needed to go inside.

"I'll be happy to come in with you or wait for you out here if you don't feel comfortable," he said.

"My grandfather is here, so I'll be fine. Thanks again for everything."

When I walked inside, Grandpa greeted me in the hallway with a hug.

"Are you all right, Pup? That was quite an ordeal."

"I'm fine. I need to get Jazzy home."

"She's already there," he said. "I took her home and fed her."

"You're the best," I said, as we walked into Designs on You. "You should get a dog or cat when you get settled in Nebraska."

"I'm not going to Nebraska."

Max, who was sitting on my desk by Tony's flowers, gave a whoop.

Smiling, Grandpa continued. "If Monica wants to stay in Abingdon, then I'll continue to date her; but she and I are a long way from the wedding chapel. I'm not about to give up my home and family for someone I'm not even sure I'd want to spend the rest of my life with."

"I knew that tomato was a manipulative so-and-so, telling Amanda she needed to consider your happiness and stand on her own two feet. 'Going to be a family.' Hmph! In her dreams!"

Grandpa laughed and shook his head. "Everybody's waiting for you at your place."

I scrunched up my nose. "Who's everybody?"

"Jason, Maggie, Dwight, and Zoe."

"That's *almost* everybody." I gave Max a pointed glance.

"You go ahead and enjoy your homecoming, darling. I'm going to rest for a while. I'll see you all tomorrow."

The next morning, Maggie and Zoe knocked on the outer door of Shops on Main before we were open.

I went and unlocked the door. "What are you guys doing here so early?"

"Aunt Max said you were here already, and we have news," Zoe said. "Plus, there's no school today because it's a teacher workday."

"Good for you!" I gave her a fist bump.

"What's your news?" Max asked. "I've been waiting to hear this for hours.

"You have not," Zoe said.

"Fine. Minutes. But those minutes felt like hours."

Zoe looked at her mom. "Go ahead. It's your news."

"Dave called Daddy last night and put a bug in his ear. Then Daddy bought Hot Diggity from Tony Diggs, and I'm going to run it." She grimaced. "Can you believe it? I'm going into the restaurant business."

She appeared nervous, but the tears gleaming in her eyes relayed her excitement.

"Congratulations," I said.

"Thanks. Will you help me learn all the ins and outs of operating a business? Being an entrepreneur is entirely new to me."

"Of course, I will."

"She's changing the name naturally," Zoe said.

"Thank goodness for that," Max said. "What's it gonna be?"

"Well, I got my love of cooking from my grandmother, so it's going to be called Dot's Diner."

Max gasped. "If that isn't just the elephant's eyebrows. My sweet Dot would be so proud of you—of all of you."

Unable to stand the heavy mood, Zoe said, "Let's get to discussing this book. Who in the world would have a set of twins and nickname them Hy and Lo?"

Author's Notes

Thank you so much for taking the time to read this book! I hope you've enjoyed it, and I'm grateful for your support and encouragement.

Victoria Holt's *Bride of Pendorric* was one of the first "grownup" mysteries I read, and I fell in love with it and then read all of Victoria Holt's books. I reread the book as I was writing this one, and it still holds up. If you haven't read it and you like gothic mysteries, check it out.

Also by Gayle Leeson

Down South Café Mystery Series

The Calamity Café

Silence of the Jams

Honey-Baked Homicide

Apples and Alibis

Fruit Baskets and Holiday Caskets

Truffles and Tragedy

Pickled to Death (Novella)

Ghostly Fashionista Mystery Series

Designs on Murder

Perils and Lace

Christmas Cloches and Corpses

Buttons and Blows

Have Yourself a Scary Little Christmas (Novella)

Secrets and Sequins

Movie Memorabilia Mystery Series

Terminated: He Won't Be Back

We'll Always Have Murder (Coming Soon!)

Literatia Series (Portal Fantasy Mystery Series written as G. Leeson)

Saving Piglet (Prequel)

An Eyre of Mystery

A Tale of Two Enemies

Kinsey Falls Chick-Lit Series

Hightail It to Kinsey Falls

Putting Down Roots in Kinsey Falls

Sleighing It in Kinsey Falls

Victoria Square Series (With Lorraine Bartlett)

Yule Be Dead

Murder Ink

Murderous Misconception

Dead Man's Hand

Tea For You (Recipe Ebook)

Embroidery Mystery Series (Written as Amanda Lee)

The Quick and The Thread

Stitch Me Deadly

Thread Reckoning

The Long Stitch Goodnight

Thread on Arrival

Cross-Stitch Before Dying

Thread End

Wicked Stitch

The Stitching Hour

Better Off Thread

Cake Decorating Mystery Series (Written as Gayle Trent)

Murder Takes the Cake

Dead Pan

Killer Sweet Tooth

Battered to Death

Killer Wedding Cake

Myrtle Crumb Mystery Series (Written as Gayle Trent)

The Party Line (short story/prequel)

Between A Clutch and a Hard Place

When Good Bras Go Bad

Claus of Death

Soup…Er…Myrtle!

Perp and Circumstance

ABOUT THE AUTHOR

Gayle Leeson is a *USA Today* bestselling, award-winning author known for infusing her stories with humor and heart. She and her family live in SW Virginia and North Carolina.

If you enjoyed this book, Gayle would appreciate your leaving a review. If you don't know what to say, there is a handy book review guide at her site (https://www.gayleleeson.com/book-review-form). Gayle invites you to sign up for her newsletter and receive excerpts of some of her books: https://forms.aweber.com/form/14/1780369214.htm

Social Media Links:
Twitter:

https://twitter.com/GayleTrent

Facebook:

https://www.facebook.com/GayleLeeson/

BookBub:

https://www.bookbub.com/profile/gayle-leeson

Goodreads:

https://www.goodreads.com/author/show/426208.Gayle_Trent

Have You Met Gia?

Excerpt from *An Eyre of Mystery*

Chapter One

Where am I? These buildings...the streets—nothing looks normal. Nothing looks modern. And the smell. Ugh. It nearly made me gag. I looked down and saw I was standing beside a pile of fresh horse dung. The horse swished its tail as it passed.

"—goa raight to t' divil then!"

"Huh?" At the sound of the brusque female voice, I raised my chin. "Are you talking to me?"

She was. Or, rather, she had been. Now the forbidding old woman dressed like she'd just stepped out of a Brontë novel shook her head, put her nose in the air, and strode on. What was that she'd said? Was it even English?

Realizing my own clothes felt a bit strange, I glanced down at the fancy, floor-length skirt I was wearing. It was a dark red satin with white and gray stripes. I imagined the bonnet tied at my throat matched it.

Am I in costume? Maybe I was in a play. No. There wouldn't be real horse dung in a play. Besides, I wasn't on a stage.

Either way, I needed to get my butt out of the middle of the road.

My mind raced as I hurried to the sidewalk. What's the last thing I remember? *I was in the library and saw that odd glowing letter L on the cover of Jane Eyre. I touched it and—*

"Now then. Come along."

It was Mr. Briggs. I knew him. I mean, I didn't know him and didn't know how I knew him, but…but I did. He was Mr. Briggs, the attorney from Jane Eyre. He led me down the macadamized street.

"Wh-what are we doing?" I asked.

"He's asked for you, and you indicated you wanted to see him." He frowned down at me. "Have you changed your mind?"

"No." I reached out and took Briggs' arm—I needed the support, but I also craved proof he was real. He was. As real as anything in this place. Had I fallen? Hit my head? Was this a dream? If so, it was the most vivid I'd ever experienced.

Briggs escorted me into a prison and spoke briefly with a jailer, who then led us to a cell. I was behind Briggs, so I couldn't see inside the cell at first.

The jailer pinched my shoulder.

I yelped in surprise and glared at him. "What was that for?"

"You don't belong here." His voice was a menacing hiss; and when he bared his teeth at me, a silverfish darted through them.

The tingling started at my scalp and worked its way through my spine. Still, I managed to lift my head slightly. I inherently knew I couldn't show this creature any hint of fear.

Briggs moved aside, and I turned away from the jailer and stepped closer to the bars.

"Edward," I whispered. Edward Rochester, the brooding hero of Jane Eyre.

"Jane. Darling, Jane." He reached for my hands through the bars.

I put my hands out, and he squeezed them.

Staring into my eyes, he said, "Wait. You aren't— He addressed Mr. Briggs then. "May we have a bit of privacy?"

"Of course. I'll be in the other room with the jailer." Mr. Briggs patted my forearm before walking away.

"Who are you?" Edward asked quietly.

"I'm Gia."

"Did Cooper send you?"

Cooper—the man who'd hired me as archivist for the Smithmore Manor library this morning.

"Yes," I said. Maybe Cooper had sent me, and maybe he hadn't, but yes seemed to be the safest answer under the circumstances.

Edward blew out a breath of relief. It wasn't pleasant. Didn't they have toothpaste in the 1840s? Gum? Mints? I'd have to look into that.

"What are you doing in prison?" I asked.

"I'm to be hanged in five days for the murder of my wife."

"Murder? No one killed Bertha. She committed suicide after setting the fire."

He shook his head. "There was no fire, and Bertha was murdered."

"You—?"

"No," he interrupted. "Not me. You need to find out who did kill her and work with Briggs to get me exonerated. I'm from your world; but if I die in this world, I'm dead in both." He paused. "Same goes for you."

I gulped. "That's good to know."

It wasn't, Reader. It wasn't good to know in the slightest.

"We have few allies here and many enemies."

"Oh, I've already made an enemy," I said. "The jailer pinched me! Then he told me I didn't belong here. And when I looked up at him, there was a silverfish in his mouth. Do you people not have toothpaste?"

"He is a silverfish. They destroy books. You're here to preserve the book—and, hopefully, my life."

"Okay, how do I—?"

"Time to go, Miss Eyre." Briggs had returned.

"Please," I said, "can't we have a few minutes more? I have so many questions."

"The jailer won't permit it. Perhaps we may return in a day or two."

"A day or two? We only have five!"

Edward pressed my hands before letting them go. "Cooper must have faith in you, so I do as well. Go and use the utmost caution."

I nodded. *What have I gotten myself into?*

Briggs helped me into a hansom cab and instructed the driver to take me to Thornfield Hall.

Thornfield Hall—the Rochester home. I tried to swallow the lump that had formed in my throat. Wonder what awaits me there?

"I have things to attend to in town, my dear, but I'll be around to check on you later this afternoon," he told me.

There weren't any silverfish in his mouth, as far as I could tell. I thanked him and was relieved for some time alone.

Taking a closer look at my outfit, I had to admit that the person who'd fashioned it had done an excellent job. It certainly felt authentic. The reticule hanging from my left wrist was gray with a floral bouquet embroidered on the front and tassels at the corners. I'd noticed the purse earlier but now took the opportunity to see what was inside—hopefully, a piece of hard candy for my uncomfortably dry mouth.

I untied the drawstring and pulled the fabric apart. Inside was a small fan, some coins, a lace-edged handkerchief, and a folded piece of tan paper. Snatching the paper out of the purse, I opened it and read:

Gia, if you're reading this, you've taken your first journey into Literatia. Congratulations! No, you aren't crazy; you aren't dreaming; you aren't comatose; you aren't dead; you aren't whatever else you might believe you are. You're actually in another world—a book world—and you must recalibrate that world before the silverfish entirely destroy the book. But no worries. I have the utmost faith in your abilities. Fond regards, Cooper Wellingham

Staring down at my employer's words, I said aloud, "This has to be a dream."

The words on the note immediately disappeared and were replaced with: *It isn't. I already told you that.*

"Wait. I can talk with you using this paper?"

Again, like some sort of weird voice-to-text device that worked in reverse or backward or upside down or something, the paper was erased, and new words appeared.

In a way. I told you when you accepted the job this morning that you were taking on a challenging role. You indicated you enjoyed challenges.

"Well, yeah, but not sci-fi, world-hopping challenges that include people with silverfish in their teeth. This is way too out of the box for me."

Had I believed you were not up to the task, I'd have never allowed you to embark upon this journey. If you aren't receptive, I need to pull you out and get someone inside who is willing to help Mr. Rochester immediately.

"I never said I wasn't willing to help Mr. Rochester." I huffed. "Of course, I am. I just—" I chewed on my lower lip for a second. "Get in here and help me already."

Unfortunately, I cannot. I'd be recognized immediately in Literatia, and the silverfish would work quickly to devour the book and everything in it. That includes Mr. Rochester and you in case you hadn't guessed.

"Mr. Rochester told me that if we die in the book, we die. Period. Am I getting hazardous duty pay for this gig? Because we never talked about my risk of dying. I figured my biggest threat would be a papercut."

Finish your task successfully, and you will be rewarded.

I wasn't making myself clear. I needed to reframe my question and stop being flippant. "What are the odds of my dying here?"

The words previously written faded out, but new words didn't come right away.

"Did you hear me?" I asked.

Low. Under all but the most extreme circumstances, I will be able to extricate you before you die.

"Oh." I slumped against my seat in relief. "And you can get Rochester out too, right?"

No. His life is in your hands.

"But he's your guy. He knew you sent me before I knew you sent me. You can't just leave him in there. In fact, why can't you take us both out of here now?"

I'm unable to remove Rochester. If I get you out, Rochester will die, and the literary classic Jane Eyre will never have existed. That has farther-reaching ramifications in our world and in Literatia than you realize. I will ask you once again, are you up to this challenge?

"I am."

Good.

"I'll keep this paper with me at all times so that I can communicate with you as necessary."

This is the only communication we can have until you return. If you were to be found with this paper, you'd be hanged as a witch.

"The last witch hanging in England took place in the late 1600s."

Trust me, they'll make an exception. Now, I'll leave you with a few words of clarification: Not everyone is who they seem or have the same personalities as those they originally embodied in the book. One of those characters killed Rochester's wife. Bring that person to justice, free Rochester, and you will be brought home. Godspeed.

Starting at one corner, the paper turned to ash. I realized Cooper was burning it on the other side. I brushed it onto the floor of the cab and watched it completely turn to dust.

This morning I'd started what I guessed would be a boring but nice job as an archivist at a gorgeous manor house in the hills of North Carolina. Now it wasn't even lunchtime, and I was responsible for a man's life, trying to avoid being killed myself, and tasked with keeping Jane Eyre safe for readers everywhere.

The cab came to a stop. I took out a coin and pulled the drawstring to close my reticule when I heard the driver climbing down from his seat.

"I thought I heard you talking," he said, upon opening the door and helping me out. "Me wife was a praying woman too."

I smiled. "Too bad she isn't here. I could use all the help I can get."

Interested in reading more? Visit my site at gayleleeson.com for more information or write me at gayle@gayleleeson.com for a five-chapter sneak peek.

www.ingramcontent.com/pod-product-compliance
Lightning Source LLC
Chambersburg PA
CBHW020324200626
46814CB00006BB/2395

* 9 7 8 1 7 3 7 3 0 0 9 9 1 *